THE FIRST BOOK OF THE

ALIENBUTT SAGA

Glenn Scrimshaw

THE WAR OF THE COFFEE BEAN

GINGERNUT BOOKS Ltd
www.gingernutbooks.co.uk

INTRODUCTION

Roswell didn't lead to the first official contact with alien life. (They've always been here. Really what I should say is official contact with post-industrial governments.) That had happened about ten years before and the most interesting facts about Roswell never even registered in the little green men theories that sprang up surrounding the crash. Those cute little alien pictures leaked out were indeed not real; they were fakes made up to hide the identity of the real passengers in the ship. Roswell was nothing more than a car crash; admittedly the car was flying and could travel through space. It was just that it crashed in a place where it shouldn't have been and it caused a bit of an interstellar incident. Another little fact you wouldn't know about the flying car was it had a little sign on it that could be turned on. When you did, that sign read "For Hire."

The passengers of this car were transferred quickly to another interstellar taxi and they left Earth after a long weekend break to what was becoming the hottest new holiday destination in the universe. Area 51, playground to the mega rich and interstellar famous. Only here could they play pranks on a semi-intelligent species that still thought itself alone in the universe, or go all rustic and hire a human body suit to live the simple life of a twentieth century human.

The driver of the taxi was never seen or mentioned in any of the theories about little green men and even though he survived the crash without a scratch his family never saw him again. He was arrested at the crash site by the interstellar police and his defense that "That bloody hill just jumped out on me," didn't work. Bigrip Alienbutt got sixty years for dangerous driving and his family was left destitute by the compensation claim made by his passengers for personal injuries sustained.

So Mrs. Alienbutt and her young hatchling Piestoff were evicted from their suburban home on the planet MZ32 and rehoused halfway across the universe in social housing on the planet Sloppystool. Moving from a planet with a number (the higher the number the better the planet) to one with a name (a burnt out rock not even worth turning into a garbage dump, so not worth a number) didn't just ruin your life, it often ended it.

Only the toughest creatures could survive for long in social housing. The crime rate was low, as you didn't survive to report a crime, and the local police were two solar systems away and only did a very fast fly past every month or so. The Alienbutts were not tough, but what they were was naturally gifted. On their home world good food had always been in short supply so they had evolved a complex digestive system which allowed them to digest any food available. This wasn't a problem until an Alienbutt started to eat rich and spicy food. The fact that this digestive system ended in four arseholes gave them a natural defence system that could take out an angry mob in under a minute at over five hundred feet distance. Alienbutts spent many years learning how to control their gas release and a skilled Alienbutt could use his gas as a weapon to match any known martial art in the universe. Not being brought up in an Alienbutt community Piestoff tended to be more a random nuclear explosion than anything like a precise weapon that could split hairs.

Piestoff's mum was no help to the young hatchling. Losing her social standing when her husband was sent to prison, and then being moved to Sloppystool had left her a broken shell of her former socialite self. Piestoff mainly brought himself up.

He teamed up with a human street urchin who lived behind the bins of his flat. She was known as the Nifty Niffler, and looking out for each other and with the help of Nifty's psychotic cat they managed to survive the rough streets.

One thing kept Piestoff going during those early years; his Uncle Stinky owned a taxi firm on the planet TW50. After his mum died when they had been on the planet for twenty years Piestoff sneaked aboard a supply ship with the only friend he had ever known, Nifty and her cat Mr. Fluffy. Finally free of the slums of Sloppystool, the universe awaited him.

But the wait was a long one. Soon caught by the crew of the ship, Piestoff and Nifty (as well as Mr. Fluffy.) were put under arrest and placed in suspended animation. One week out from Sloppystool the ship mysteriously disappeared for six hundred years. When it was found, only three survivors remained. The story made big news on Earth. It turned out Nifty and her cat had been abducted by unknown alien genetic scientists from late twentieth century Earth. Deported from Sloppystool for having no valid immigration papers, she returned to Earth a celebrity. Now not only was she the oldest living human, but also the genetic experiments carried out on her had given her super human reflexes and strength. Those same experiments on Mr. Fluffy had made a super intelligent cat that plotted to reclaim its universe that rightfully belonged to him. Luckily for the universe he was still in a cat's body and his paws couldn't work the technology needed for him to achieve his aims.

His murderous psychotic tendencies were only held in check to protect his favourite belonging, Nifty. Piestoff he didn't much care for, as he smelled bad. So Mr. Fluffy plotted in secret, hiding his intelligence from all, just waiting for his chance to strike and claim the universe for his own.

CHAPTER 1

The Taxi years.

INTERSTELLAR NEWS CHANNEL 9.
NEWS FLASH.

The price of coffee beans rocketed to a new high today as news of a bad crop in the Rata System came to light. Rata is the sixth largest producer of coffee in the galaxy, and the news triggered large scale rioting in several systems that depend on Rata coffee for their supply. The Coffee Houses based on Earth have moved to quell fears of rationing in a statement made to the Federation Senate.

Alienbutt had grown up on Sloppystool dreaming of following in his father's footsteps and being a taxi driver. It was a family tradition going back seven generations. Also for someone with no formal education it was a fast way to earn the money needed to enter the Federation Academy to become a starship commander. Piestoff Alienbutt had big plans, which true to form hadn't worked. Because of several centuries spent in suspended animation he was now too old to enrol in the academy by about six hundred years, but he did get his taxi. The Interstellar mk5 taxi cab had originally been designed as a military drop ship. It could hold up to ten persons and had the ability to be launched from large deep space troop ships safe at the edge of a system. From there it could fly to its target planet and then was able to navigate in the planet's atmosphere. Five million had been built by the Chrom military for a war against the Ji Hunters, a race of intergalactic reprobates renowned for causing trouble and stealing anything that caught their eye. As the Chrom massed to attack, the sneaky Ji Hunters nerve gassed the entire fleet ending the war before a Chrom managed to shoot a gun in anger. The captured fleet was then sold off by the Ji and an enterprising fellow bought some of the drop ships and put taxi meters in them. They quickly became the cab of choice for the short distance cabbie with over twelve hundred thousand now flying around "For Hire."

So Piestoff had achieved half of his childhood ambition but quickly he had set himself a new goal as the reality of his life set in. This time he set himself a real grown up goal and not some boyhood fantasy. The first part of his plan was to be anything else apart from a taxi driver. How he hated his bloody taxi, always in the repair bay having worn out parts replaced in a never ending cycle of expenses. When the stupid thing did work he would spend his days and nights picking up customers who were not interesting and full of the joys of space, but more often unhappy and dull, all eager for their next fix of coffee.

He had expected to be trawling the galaxy going from one system to the next, dodging space pirates and asteroid storms. Instead he got shoppers heading for the off planet retail parks and hyper markets with the odd job to the hyper jump station, where you could be on the other side of the galaxy in a matter of minutes for the equivalent of five years of Alienbutt's annual income. The invention of the hyper jump had overnight destroyed the interstellar business class taxi trade. Now it was all local work, you never left the system.

Sloopystool had changed so much from his childhood days. It was now the largest producer of coffee in the universe and social housing was a distant memory. Five hundred years before, humans had entered space and brought coffee with them. To almost all other species coffee was highly addictive, even the smell of it could get some species hooked. The coffee revolution had quickly made humanity the major player in the universe and within fifty years earth companies had taken over almost everything worth buying.

Sloppystool's climate was so similar to Earth's that now ninety percent of the planet's landmass was turned over to coffee production. The population of the planet now lived in giant floating cities situated on the planet's oceans and most worked on the coffee farms or associated companies. With the off planet shopping centres, Sloppystool had become a major trading centre where people could make a fortune, if they didn't become addicted to coffee, which was now used not just for drinking but in foods, chewing gum and even perfume. Almost the whole universe was a captive to the coffee companies' marketing departments. Only humans, the aloof Ick Empire and a certain alien race with four arseholes were immune to the little brown bean.

Piestoff threw himself into taxi driving, working long hours to earn the money to buy passage to anywhere and buy a home when he got there. He had his plan and was desperate to make it happen. But while Alienbutts couldn't become addicted to things, they could grow to like things with a passion that could become obsessive. Piestoff really obsessively liked spicy kebabs and whiskey, and would often fly over to the next planet Hardstool to buy whiskey to last him a month, then drink it all over the weekend while eating kebab after kebab. Because of this his savings never really grew. After a weekend blowout he would start again, working longer hours until he could bear it no longer and he would have another weekend blowout.

Piestoff would spend most of his time at work sat in his Interstellar mk5 taxi waiting. Being a taxi driver you learnt how to wait like an expert. Waiting over an hour between jobs was normal and Control, who gave out the jobs would give him crap; often it wasn't even going off planet. But on this particular day the job had a pet. He hated animals and they hated him. Control knew this and still the slimeball gave him jobs with pets. The only way to get good jobs from Control was to be his friend, to go out drinking with him, buying his drinks. This job though, would have a massive impact on Piestoff's future.

He looked at the job again.

2436 Shorepond street, Sector 4, Newport City.
Lady and a Mutthound puppy.
Going to sector 32, Shazzer town.

Growing up on Sloppystool in the pre-coffee days Piestoff's only experience of animals apart from Mr. Fluffy was the now extinct two foot red beetles that made up the main diet of the planet's populace. Even heavily spiced they tasted horrid, and more people died from food poisoning than from any other cause. This had left his experience with animals limited to one evil cat and food that often killed you.

The pick-up point was a good thirty minutes away in an area he wouldn't usually go into after dark unless he had a full squad of riot marines with him. Taking off from his parking spot he pulled into the traffic, causing two other ships to swerve to avoid colliding with him. There followed the usual hand signals and cursing, but what did they expect? He drove a taxi after all and the usual rules of driving didn't apply to taxi drivers. Driving in-orbit on Sloppystool was one of the most dangerous jobs you could do,, as traffic came from any direction and you had to keep your reflexes sharp or your second to last journey ever would be much shorter than you planned, and once you had been scraped up you would start your final journey.

Before long, Piestoff was landing outside the run-down building. He got out of his seat and pressed the button to open the rear doors. His fare was a young Belguin female. She looked very similar to the humans but the Belguins had purple skin and seven fingers. She stood waiting at the back of the taxi with four large bags.

"Hi love could you just store these while I get Poodle?, They did say I had a puppy, didn't they?" She smiled then quickly turned and went around the back of the house. Piestoff grabbed the first two bags and put them into the storage locker then went back for the other two. As he walked back up the ramp into his taxi he heard a low growl. Looking around he saw nothing so walked to the locker and put the bags in. As he closed the lid he felt something breathing on the back of his neck. He looked down to see two large clawed paws next to his own feet. Very slowly he turned around to

5

look into two large orange eyes and a large mouth full of lots of large sharp teeth. A long tongue lolled out of the side of the mouth, dripping drool. The rest of the body was covered in long black fur, and there was a lot of body there.

From the doorway he heard the ladies voice. "Poodles put down the nice taxi man." The beast sniffed him, which would normally cause anything to at least run off whimpering, as Piestoff was nervous and two of his arseholes were really testing the charcoal butt plugs he wore at work. Instead it licked his face and went to lay down behind the driver's seat.

"Oh that's lovely, he likes you, Mr. Taxi man." The girl smiled as she walked past to sit in the passenger seat. Piestoff stood transfixed for a moment longer, then wiping the drool off his face, edged himself into the driver's seat.

"They said you had a puppy." Piestoff cast a quick look at the six foot monster. "A mutthound?"

"He is, he's only six month old, they grow to be at least twelve foot, could you stop off at the pet world on Pond Alley? I need to get him a snack to stop him getting hungry, did you know...."

Piestoff switched off and headed for the pet world, the girl had a voice that grated and the word hungry made him nervous. She droned on as he flew while Poodles moved its head to rest next to Piestoff's foot.

Two minutes later Piestoff landed his taxi outside the pet shop. The girl jumped up and headed for the rear door.

"Poodles, stay! I'll only be a minute love, if he gets playful just smack him on the nose." With that she disappeared down the ramp.

After half an hour Piestoff called in the job. "Control, I've had a runner."

"Piestoff me old mate, did you not get any credits up front?" Control as usual was being that smug git you wanted to smack. Biting back what he wanted to say to the slimy fat slug, Piestoff looked into the face of Poodles who now sat next to him panting and looking hungry. "They left their puppy as security, I will drop it onto the base," said Piestoff hopefully.

"Can't do that mate. You'll have to keep hold of it until we sort it out." Control had gone from smug to this is your problem smug without missing a beat.

"I will have to take you off duty till it's sorted, sorry mate".

Like hell was he sorry, he would already be laughing his arse off. With certainty Piestoff knew the house would be empty and the phone number fake. He was stuck with this beast that had now started to chew on the passenger seat. By law he couldn't get rid of it for two months when if the taxi fare wasn't paid it would become his. What the hell was he going to do with a six foot plus walking fur rug with the build of a space troll? At least she had left four bags of puppy food in his lockers. That should last a day or so.

Piestoff had been stuck looking after Poodles for about a month. He couldn't leave him at his home as he wailed and ate the metal furniture, so for want of anything better to do he brought him to work with him. Piestoff would now work for up to eighteen hours a day and in that time would drink at least seven cups of coffee. While to most intelligent life forms coffee was addictive and most would now be needing a detox course to stop them bouncing off the walls, to Alienbutts it tasted nice and beat the fizzy drinks you normally got at the burger drive-through (which gave him even worse gas.) Taxi drivers the universe over love drive-through burger bars. You can get food and drink and you don't have to get out of your taxi and miss the job of the night. Plus the job title was taxi driver which means you drive, you never walk; it's against your work ethic.

Having to look after Poodles, who had almost doubled in size over the last month, Piestoff was now working an extra four hours a day just to feed him. But having an eleven foot plus Mutthound sat by the back door discouraged people from not paying and also made for very good tips from nervous punters. Poodles was starting to grow on him and didn't seem to mind the natural odor that surrounded Piestoff, also he didn't seem to drool quite so much now.

In fact Piestoff's standing with his fellow taxi drivers had gone up no end when a few days before four Trollian gangsters had tried to rob a fellow driver. Piestoff had been first to arrive to help out when the Alpha call had gone out. (An Alpha call was a quick and polite way of saying. "Help, some no good low life is trying to bash out my brains and the police take an hour to turn up while thirty taxis are there in half that time with various tools to cause damage to the little shits"). Poodles had gone through the gang of eight foot Trollians, and had them begging for mercy within thirty seconds. After that they had paid their intended victim the fare owed plus a large tip for the stress caused and the word was out. Don't mess with the Sloppystool taxi drivers, they've got a new weapon to protect them. For the first time Piestoff was accepted by the other drivers and Control even started to give him the odd good job.

Piestoff had been taxi driving for about two years before he was finally considered experienced enough for working the planet Hardstool. It was always a gamble, your first job on Hardstool; you either did the job and got paid or you got a memorial plaque at the office. Piestoff though had fitted right in with the locals, a shared love of junk food and strong drink bridging the cultural gap. Hardstool was a terraformed planet that had been colonized by humans, mainly the New Lothians.

The old Highlanders of Scotland had moved into exile after Scotland became a giant amusement park centred around Loch Ness. A large aquatic beast was imported from some distant planet that acted as the legendary monster. This beast soon hunted down and killed the shy and secretive real Nessy. The Highlanders soon settled into their new home on Hardstool and now produced the finest Scotch whiskey in the universe, just as Sloopystool produced the finest Brazilian coffee.

The planet was more run by street gangs than anyone else and the most feared of them was 'The Ladies' Darts Team.' This gang consisted of Claire and Mary the six foot muscle, Stacey and Debs and finally the leader, the four foot Killashandra. They ran the largest protection racket on the planet but as they were always drunk they hired taxis when they went out collecting. Killashandra was unique in New Lothian society as she didn't like the taste of whiskey. This was normally a hanging offence. By the age of sixteen, though, she had over forty sporrans nailed to her door frame from people who had tried to place a noose over her head, so the matter was dropped and never mentioned again.

The girls were regular customers with the taxi firm but now always asked for Piestoff. This was so Claire could play with Poodles. The first time they had met she had held him down and put a pink ribbon in his hair. Poodles was so scared after that he now sat still and let her. For Piestoff the street gang had become the closest thing to friends he had known since Nifty had gone. The girls liked him because he would match them drink for drink and was the only person ever to win a drinking contest against Stacey, when after four days of drinking he had challenged her to drink a double shot of his special recipe chilli sauce. Stacey had woken up two days later unable to speak because of the burns in her mouth. But like all good things in Piestoff's life, just as he started to get used

9

to them, things would go wrong.

Now Piestoff was parked around the corner from the bar "The Wembley Goal Posts." An odd name, but Debs had explained it was named after a daring raid by Scottish patriots in the late 20th century where they had looted the posts from under the noses of their old enemy the English.

Looking through his mirror he saw the girls stagger around the corner. He started to lower the rear door ramp as the girls broke into a run. Pretty soon a large angry mob of kilted Highlands also rounded the corner giving chase. Piestoff was starting to take off as the last of the girls jumped onto the ramp. Pressing the ramp lift button he shot into the traffic two hundred feet above. Killashandra slumped into the chair next to Piestoff breathing heavily.

"Thanks, Piestoff, you'll never guess what that daft cow's done?" She jerked her thumb in the direction of Stacey who had already lit up a cigarette. "She's only gone and nicked the Wembley goal post!" Piestoff looked blankly first at Killashandra then Stacey who sheepishly pulled a three foot section of white post from behind her back.

"The actual Wembley goal post, it's priceless, we're rich." She slurred.

"We're dead you daft cow, everyone on Hardstool will be after us now."

Piestoff felt pressure build on the cork in arsehole number three; if Killashandra was worried then Piestoff was scared.

"Where to now?" he stammered.

"Head for Starbase Maxwell please, I need time to work out how we live to see tomorrow." Piestoff jumped lanes causing a minor collision behind him as he headed off into the upper orbit. It wouldn't take long for word to get out, so Piestoff wanted to be off planet quick.

Starbase Maxwell was one of two deep space trading posts

where deep space ships would constantly be passing through. As Piestoff came into sight of it he noticed two things, firstly there were three large Ick dreadnoughts moored at the station and secondly there was the unmistakable black custom starship of the Ick playboy leader, Wickede. The Ick were the only people able to withstand the advance of the Earth coffee houses, and now stood as the only independent group of any worth in the whole universe. They didn't have the coffee bean but what they did have was the best technology and ship designs. The dreadnought was the most powerful ship in space; it was a nuclear missile compared to everyone else's hand grenade. Killashandra pointed to a spare docking bay next to the Ick starships. "Drop us off there, Piestoff." She looked over her shoulder. "Make yourselves lovely girls. I've got a great plan."

Piestoff set back off towards Hardstool with a large tip and the white post secured in the hold. Life wasn't as short as it had been ten minutes ago but it wouldn't be as much fun. Again Piestoff was getting left behind, but Killashandra refused to put him in any more danger despite his pleading to go with them. As he started his final approach towards Hardstool the proximity alarm on his taxi went off. Not knowing where the threat came from he covered his head with his arms, which all things considered was totally pointless. Looking through his fingers he saw the black Ick starship pass him by, quickly followed by a police pursuit ship. The Ick ship flirted with the upper atmosphere of Hardstool in a display that caused flames to shoot along its length and its hull to glow red before executing a ninety degree turn and shooting off into space and jumping to light speed.

Piestoff fought to control his taxi as it was buffeted by the cosmic waves caused by the ship's jump to light speed. Finally gaining control he saw the police pursuit ship had suffered the same fate as his ship. He quickly flipped the switch of his radio to the police scanner channel.

"...Jumped to light speed guv. We lost em."

"OK, we'll put out an all point on the stolen ship. Now, find that taxi that dropped them off."

Piestoff decided life was going to be very short again. As the pursuit ship turned around to face him, the pressure on his corks began to build.

Piestoff had been sitting in the small interview room for hours. First they had been nice and given him a cup of coffee and biscuits as they took his statement. Then they had left him alone and another police officer had come in with two bruisers who stayed by the door. This time when Piestoff gave the same answers, there had been shouting and threats. Finally the police man had picked up the empty coffee cup and thrown it at the wall. The coffee cup retaliated by bouncing back and hitting him full in the face. With blood pouring from his broken nose, the policeman had stormed out to get medical attention.

That had been ages ago, but now things changed. In walked a tall human who oozed style from every pore, from his black sunglasses to his impossibly shiny black boots. This guy wasn't police, he was far too stylish and dangerous looking. Behind him, a much shorter man in an equally expensive suit and sunglasses stumbled to the chair and sat down. He removed his glasses to reveal the bleary eyes of one who was royally hungover. The first figure stayed lurking near the door. His sardonic expression was highlighted by a goatee beard and Alienbutt re-evaluated 'dangerous' to 'apex hunter dangerous'. The small guy cleared his throat and Piestoff's eyes returned to him. For a fraction of a second he saw a cold cunning intelligence before the look of a man with a hangover returned.

"We believe your story and the police will be releasing you soon." Piestoff knew the man by the door was a killer, but the small guy told him who to kill. With a warm smile he stood up. "This is my employee Blackarachnia who has agreed to get my ship back, but before he sets off he's going to help you return the wooden post to Hardstool where you will get a hero's welcome no doubt."

Piestoff's corks took another battering; Blackarachnia, the most feared bounty hunter in the galaxy. Then after sitting in shock for long enough to look stupid, a second wave hit him.

"Your ship? But that means that you're..."

"Wickede." He shoved out his hand, a wide grin on his face. "Just call me Wickede, all my friends do."

Poodles lay sleeping still, the police had sedated him so they could search the ship, but not before twelve officers had needed a total of seven thousand stitches from the over-protective Mutthound that hadn't wanted strangers aboard Alienbutt's taxi. Piestoff, still in shock, sat in the driver's seat while beside him sat Blackarachnia. Wickede had waved them off and promised to come and visit now they were friends. His composure was close to shattering and he still had to return the Wembley goal post to a planet-wide angry lynch mob. Then he was home to get drunk for a month; this was all too much for him.

"Hey man, can I ask you a question?"

Piestoff jumped as this was the first time Blackarachnia had spoken. Not trusting his voice Piestoff nodded.

"I read your file and it says you're a childhood friend of the Nifty Niffler."

Again Piestoff nodded. Nifty had been his only friend but had been deported back to Earth when it was discovered she had been a victim of alien abduction, so had no papers to be on Sloppystool. On all accounts she was rich and famous now. Piestoff decided he would need a new cork suspender belt, this one was taking too much of a hammering.

"I met her at this society party on earth two months back, but she won't return my calls. How can I get her to go out on a date with me?"

The cork butt plugs failed as Piestoff finally lost all rational thought. The cork plugs shot straight through his chair and embedded themselves in the steel floor, steaming and half melted.

"Geez man, I think you need some clean pants," choked Blackarachnia as he scrambled for the oxygen mask above his chair, but Piestoff didn't hear him as he sank into a deep well of madness.

Piestoff opened his eyes and looked up at the sky. High up he could make out the traffic flying about as life on Sloppystool went on. A bad dream, that must be what had happened. His hand grasped at the grass he was laid on and pulling up a hand full of the soft well cut blades, he held them to his face and sniffed in the fresh clean smell... of smoke. Sitting up he looked around to see he was laid in the centre circle of a giant sports arena, not on Sloppystool, but the Hardstool International Sports Arena. The main stand was on fire and he was sure his taxi was right in the centre of the blaze that was rapidly turning into an inferno. Blackarachnia walked into view, brushing dust from the shoulders of his ripped overcoat, but still wearing his black sunglasses.

"I think it's time to leave. Good luck man, but I couldn't save the post, and your pet's run off God knows where." Lifting up his right arm he prepared to speak into his wrist com.

"Wait! You can't leave me here," pleaded Piestoff.

"Why? Wickede asked me to see you back to the planet. I've done that," answered Blackarachnia. The bounty hunter hadn't got where he was by doing random acts of kindness, in fact he had never done any acts of kindness, plenty of acts of violence, just not kindness.

"Why? They'll kill me. Not only have I destroyed the Wembley goal post but I crashed into their sports' arena. This is where Hardstool F.C. won the Galactic Worlds' Championship when Doug McDougal scored a hat trick. It's the very core of all things Hardstool." Panic didn't just edge Piestoff's voice, it oozed from every pore of his being. Blackarachnia shrugged his shoulders, not really caring in the slightest and continued to speak to his wrist com. Then he paused and looked at the terrified taxi driver.

"Two to beam up, looks like we got a new cleaner for the ship, and get a lock on his dog too. Beam that thing into the brig." The two figures seemed to be viewed through a heat haze and then disappeared just as the fuel tanks on Piestoff's taxi exploded, destroying a large section of the north stand and spreading sheets of fire that engulfed the rest of the stadium.

On board the Ick dreadnought, Wickede stood watching as Blackarachnia's ship left Hardstool's orbit. Next to him stood Snoodgrass, his first adviser and closest friend.

"Well if the prophecy is right, we now know four of the ten who will support the Nexus," said Wickede still staring after the vanished ship.

"Wickede, if we have to put our faith in that Alienbutt," Snoodgrass trailed off to silence.

Turning from the ship's window Wickede smiled.

"Two years ago you thought I was a waste of space and Blackarachnia a heartless killer, now we are your champions. Give him a chance, I like him, but you must invent one of your

15

gadgets, because his butts seriously stink." Wickede walked over to a table and poured two whiskeys.

"Blackarachnia is a heartless killer who works for you only because you pay the most; he cares nothing for our cause and has never done a good deed in his life. What if this Alienbutt isn't the one? With you and your companions there is enough in the prophecy to work out who you are. The chosen one is outside those predictions and can change the way the future will be written. It is all guesswork and hoping he works to help our cause," pressed Snoodgrass.

"Still invent something to make him smell better." Smiling, he passed over a drink. "Without him the Ick will be destroyed, with him we stand a chance, and Blackarachnia helped the Alienbutt so that's a good deed right there."

Piestoff Alienbutt finally got to leave the Sloppystool system but didn't realising that Fate and Destiny had forgotten about him. They had built a whole game that he wasn't invited to play, yet the rest of their family were doing their best to sneak him in through the back door. So now he was the central player as the Ick made plans to prevent a terrible future. He was the chosen, a person without a destiny, able to make it up as he went along. The whole future of the universe was about to be thrown into the mixing bowl of chance as Alienbutt became the mixing spoon that would churn it up. To say the destiny of kings rode on his shoulders would just mean a few million souls, as kings had mainly fallen out of fashion the universe over. It would be better to say on his shoulder rode a little brown bean, plus the addicted souls of a million worlds and every move he made would cause changes as to how the universe should unfold.

CHAPTER 2

The Book of Ick.

INTERSTELLAR NEWS CHANNEL 9.
NEWS FLASH.

The Federation Senate today granted new powers to the coffee producers to remove populations from planets suitable for coffee bean production. Any terraformed planet with less than one thousand years of history could now be converted as the great coffee bean drought continues to bite. Production on eight of the thirty planet production centres have dropped over the last few years, leading to universal unrest. Conspiracy theories that the Coffee Houses are stockpiling massive amounts of the bean to bring about the crisis have been rubbished.

In other news, a scientist who claimed to have isolated the protein that makes the coffee bean so addictive has been found dead after coffee addicts broke into his facility to steal his supply of test beans. The facility was burnt down during the robbery and all research lost. The Coffee Houses that sponsored his research have not yet commented on how security was breached.

ONE YEAR LATER.

Three single seater run-abouts raced through the asteroid field dodging around the giant rocks that slowly spun, collided and spun back in an endless cycle of movement. Piestoff, who piloted one of the three, was much changed from the taxi driver who had left Sloppystool in such a hurry. Blackarachnia who had hired him to be the ship's cleaner had spent much of his time teaching Piestoff to fly all manner of spaceships, everything from the little run-abouts they were flying now to the large starships used for deep space travel. The two had become firm friends. This was something that puzzled Blackarachnia as he had never before wanted or needed friendship. He realised that there was something about the strange smelly Alienbutt that was causing a change in how he viewed the universe. Blackarachnia had a natural gift for killing that he had taken full advantage of, but in the company of Alienbutt he was different. He now felt more alive than ever before and for the first time he had started to care about things. After a visit to Earth to see Nifty, who had now joined them on Blackarachnia's flagship, the three had become totally inseparable. Blackarachnia had a whole new set of strange feelings to confuse him that centred around Nifty, and he wasn't sure what they meant.

For the first time in his life Piestoff felt happy and safe amongst friends. Always an outsider, Piestoff had grown up unsure of himself and doubting his every move. Now that he had discovered some confidence from feeling he belonged, he had grown into himself. Without even realising it, both Piestoff and Nifty were being trained by Blackarachnia to survive in a large hostile universe. They were being taught not to be victims but to survive the only way Blackarachnia knew how. Both were natural pilots, Nifty having enhanced reflexes and Piestoff's time spent dodging the traffic as a taxi driver, giving them an aptitude for combat flying that no amount of training could achieve. In Blackarachnia's world it was kill or be killed and he would ensure the strange fat arsed alien and the captivating Nifty would not be lacking in any skill he could teach them.

A collision of two giant rocks ahead caused one of the rocks to split and a piece larger than their ships whirled dangerously towards their three ships. Nifty, in the lead ship, banked sharply and easily avoided the danger. Blackarachnia who lagged slightly behind the other two climbed sharply over the top of the rocks but Piestoff had no room to play with. Without thinking he opened fire, sending four torpedoes into the rock and blindly flying through the explosion that cleared his way to safety.

With alarms and buzzers going off as fragments of rock battered the little ship, Piestoff eased off the accelerator and pulled up to get free of the asteroids and into clear space.

"Bugger!" shouted Piestoff as he struggled to control the damaged ship as the controls failed.

"You OK Alienbutt, you look a little cooked?" Blackarachnia voice came through the com. link as he pulled his own ship clear of the asteroid field and circled back towards the now stationary Piestoff.

"Lost most of my lateral thrusters and my shields are fried but those new butt-plugs that Wickede sent are holding up a treat." Piestoff replied in a matter of fact way that he would have found impossible just a few months before. If he was making Blackarachnia more emotional, then Blackarachnia was making him more detached, the two personalities rubbing off on each other to make them both complete. Nifty's ship came racing back doing a victory roll as she dodged the

19

asteroids with ease.

"I win again boys."

"You been tinkering with your ship again. It's faster than ours," responded Blackarachnia gruffly, but both Nifty and Piestoff knew his face would be split by a huge grin. Nifty's laughter rang out as she performed the equivalent of a handbrake turn to end up nose to nose with Blackarachnia's ship. Pausing for long enough to wave, she then reversed and spun the ship again.

"I'll go get someone to give Piestoff a tow, and good shooting Piestoff, you really nailed that rock." With that she spun her ship again and hit the thrusters and was gone.

"Blackarachnia, if I was you I would just admit she's a better pilot than us and let her rub our noses in it for a bit," Alienbutt put in as he flicked switches trying to regain the use of the ship.

Blackarachnia laughed. "True, she's one of the best pilots I've ever seen."

"Only one of the best?" asked Piestoff.

"You haven't seen Wickede fly yet, that's a race I wouldn't bet on."

Piestoff cleared his throat. "I've been meaning to ask about Wickede. Won't he be a little annoyed that you haven't been searching for his stolen ship?" Piestoff was worried about Killashandra and the girls and the fact that Blackarachnia was supposed to be searching for them in order to recover it.

"Don't worry about your friends, Piestoff. If Wickede wanted them dead he would activate the homing beacon or the self-destruct on the ship. For some reason he's not that bothered. He probably found it funny having a group of chicks steal his ship." Blackarachnia moved his ship alongside Piestoff's. "Come on let's get that pile of junk moving in the right direction, and you're buying the drinks tonight for wrecking another of my ships."

Piestoff groaned and turned his attention to nursing his ship back to Blackarachnia's dreadnought. Another evening in the bar watching Blackarachnia and Nifty making eyes at each other. Human courtship was strange, but at least there was plenty of drink to be had while he played gooseberry.

Blackarachnia burst into Piestoff's sleeping quarters, poured a drink of water and kicked the bunk with the sleeping Piestoff on. "Come on man! It's the afternoon already."

Piestoff opened one eye and wondered why he couldn't see. After a moment's panic he realised and peeled a half-eaten naan bread off his face, the remains of last night's kebab. He looked up to see Blackarachnia looming over him holding out the cup of water, sitting up he reached out a shaking hand to take it. His head instantly started to pound as his hangover woke up and screamed within his head. He took the glass and drank it in one, then put his head in his hands to hold it together as it threatened to split apart. Yet again he'd had too much to drink in the bar and now he had to suffer the consequences. Suddenly without warning Blackarachnia leaned forward and put a hypodermic medisyringe against his neck and pressed the button. A quick sting and it delivered a liquid direct into Alienbutt's bloodstream and his hangover vanished.

"Why can't you ever let me enjoy my hangovers for a few hours?" whined Piestoff rubbing his neck knowing his chances of spending another few hours in bed were now zero.

"Because I'm a vicious thug, now come on and get cleaned up, we just received orders so it's time to earn some money." Blackarachnia walked over to a small sink area and wet a cloth which he threw over to Alienbutt who caught it and wiped his face.

"We're meeting up with Wickede and an Ick fleet and

then we're going for a big bounty out in the outer quadrants. Seems someone's been pillaging the wrong outposts and the Federation have had enough. We need to get there fast as there will be bounty hunters from all over heading for this one as the pay's good."

A light switched on in Piestoff's head. "I take it you're not wanting me along as the ship's cleaner then. Have you promoted me and forgotten to mention it?"

Blackarachnia grinned "I want two wing men I can trust, Nifty's already agreed." He left the statement hanging while Piestoff gazed at the floor taking in the news that he had suspected subconsciously for a while.

"What if I freeze on you or run away?" Piestoff finally whispered.

"If you run away you'll owe me big time and you won't freeze as the onboard ship's heaters are great. If anything you'll want to open a window as it'll be too warm."

"I'm serious Blackarachnia." Piestoff looked up and stared into Blackarachnia's smiling face, feeling scared and uncertain.

"Speak to Wickede tonight Piestoff, he's better with words than me."

Both looked down as a scraping noise came from under Piestoff's bunk. Poodles crawled out and unfolded himself to stand towering over Blackarachnia, cocking his head to one side he stood as if waiting an answer to a question.

"Mr. Fluffy is still in Nifty's quarters so you're safe to go get breakfast," said Blackarachnia as he reached up and patted Poodles on the shoulder. As if understanding, the Mutthound dropped to all fours and padded out in search of food.

"How can something so big be afraid of a little cat?" mused Blackarachnia.

"Everyone apart from Nifty is scared of Fluffy and your security officer says if he pisses in his boots one more time he's gonna quit on you and find a desk job," answered Piestoff pulling on his own boots, standing up he started to swear.

"That bloody cat, he's pissed in mine too, again!"

Blackarachnia shook his head and walked out of the cabin laughing. "I'll catch you down on the bridge when you find your spare pair."

After a quick search of his quarters Piestoff found his spare boots also sitting in a puddle of Mr. Fluffy's making. Cursing he ran down to the ship's spares stores and lost property to find anything he could put on. After a frantic ten minutes search, Piestoff stepped out of the stores room hoping no one would notice his borrowed boots. They were bright patent red and knee high with more silver buckles than was good and a four inch platform sole. He had never noticed the stores' keeper before, a strange guy called Ensign Fashion. He had picked out the boots saying they were the only ones in Alienbutt's size and for the life of him, Alienbutt couldn't remember what the Ensign looked like. Today he just knew it was going to be one of those days that happened to him far too often. Making his way to the bridge he prepared himself for the comments that were bound to come.

Piestoff stood waiting nervously in the hanger-bay with Nifty and Blackarachnia. Wickede's shuttle was just entering through the bay doors. Blackarachnia had only laughed for about half an hour at the boots and now stood softly giggling whenever he looked down at Piestoff's feet. Nifty had kept a better control of herself but couldn't keep the smirk from her face. The shuttle landed before them and the door slid open. Wickede started to walk out, then stopped, he looked at Piestoff then at his feet, then at Blackarachnia who was again in danger of losing control of himself and making strangled chuckling noises, Nifty looked away, furiously coughing behind an upraised hand and not wanting to make eye contact with the new arrivals.

"Was there a fancy dress party last night?" he asked, unable to take his eyes off the boots.

Blackarachnia doubled over, tears streaming down his face while even Nifty lost control and couldn't help but laugh.

"The cat pissed in my boots," answered Piestoff. He turned and stormed off. Behind him the sound of a fresh round of laughter followed him.

Piestoff was half way to the bridge when he heard running feet behind him. He turned around to see the short form of an Ick running to catch up. In truth he wasn't angered by Blackarachnia's laughing at his boots. He knew how ridiculous they looked. What was bothering him was the fact that he was supposed to be going into a fight, with guns, and he hadn't done that before. Piestoff was scared as the other side would have guns too and despite the many bar brawls he had been in, no one had ever actually shot at him.

The Ick came to a stop before him and saluted. "Commander Alienbutt, could you join Wickede and Captain Blackarachnia in the Captain's office?"

"What? I'm not, I don't have a rank, I'm not a commander, more just the cleaner really." Piestoff looked confused but started to follow the Ick as he headed on towards the bridge and Blackarachnia's office that was just next to it. He would be there before the others and have to wait.

"I think you may find that Wickede may have given you the rank, a sort of title for services to the Ick."

"I haven't done anything for the Ick," said an even more confused Piestoff. "You're only the second Ick I've ever spoken to."

"You haven't helped the Ick yet but you will. I'm Commander Snoodgrass, or just Snoodgrass and I've done bugger all too to get a rank, and I'm sure you'll meet many more of our people before long." He grinned and pulled out a hip flask, took a quick drink and passed it to Piestoff. "Single malt whiskey, works well to stop you getting nervous."

"I just use it to get drunk," shrugged Piestoff. He took a longer drink. "But if it can stop me being," he paused, "nervous, I could get used to using it for that job too." Piestoff handed the flask back to Snoodgrass a good deal more empty than when he took it. "That's good stuff you got, much better than I usually drink."

Snoodgrass grinned. "The secret is to block out the nervous part of you but stay alert. I always have a nip or two before any big event, a trick I learnt from Wickede." They reached the door to Blackarachnia's office, and rather than wait Snoodgrass went right in. Piestoff paused a second and then followed. The office was dominated by a table and twelve large chairs. Going to one end of the table Snoodgrass started to press on the table before five of the chairs so that small monitor screens popped up from the smooth table surface. "If you sit next to me during the meeting I'll explain anything you miss later on." Walking over to the wall he switched on the sensor viewer screen and Piestoff looked at the Ick fleet that came into view on it. Five dreadnoughts had met up with Blackarachnia's ship and now stood waiting. Piestoff wandered over to the screen and looked out into space while Snoodgrass slumped into a chair.

"How's your bum-plugs working out, if you don't mind me asking?"

Piestoff turned around grinning. "Great, I haven't had a leak since Wickede sent them to me, the best gift I've ever had."

"I'm glad they work, I had to work from bits of old information that escaped your home world's destruction, but very little escaped on how to make the bum-plugs so I wasn't sure how well they would hold up."

"You made them?" Piestoff looked shocked and came to sit by Snoodgrass, who looked embarrassed.

"Wickede asked me to after you met him on Sloppystool." He had the good grace not to mention the fact that when his old butt-plugs had failed he had almost killed Blackarachnia, but had managed to destroy a major landmark on the planet Hardstool. The old butt-plugs had never worked that well anyway. They always left an aroma around Piestoff that kept most people at a distance.

Further conversation was stopped as the door slid open and Wickede entered followed by Blackarachnia and Nifty. This was a different Wickede to the one Piestoff remembered from the police interview room. The crumpled, hungover playboy was replaced by a confident leader who knew what was going on. Taking a seat at the head of the table, Blackarachnia and Nifty sat opposite Piestoff and Snoodgrass.

"Alienbutt it's good to see you again. Nifty explained about your footwear problem but we can catch up properly later. Our little fleet will be setting off for the Omiga five sector with all speed, so transport between ships will be impossible for the two days while we are at light speed, so that's plenty of time to share a few drinks."

"So what's the job Wickede; six dreadnoughts is overkill for even the largest criminal band out there?" asked Blackarachnia.

"O.K. Blackarachnia we'll go straight to business. Snoodgrass could you explain to our friends what's happening?" answered Wickede.

Snoodgrass sat back in his chair and was silent for a moment composing what to say.

"The Outer Systems have always been a hideout for pirates and others who operate outside the Federation laws. Having no standing armies and a law enforcement force that can't cope with even the inner systems, keeping order out there has always fallen to local governors and the bounty hunters. Larger colonies have had defences strong enough to repel these mainly disorganised bands, but over the last few months several large colonies have been destroyed. From the reports that we have received, it appears that those bands have united and become organised. In response to those reports, bounty hunters will be gathering ready for a combined offensive."

"It won't work, Wickede, bounty hunters work alone or in small groups." Blackarachnia got to his feet and walked over to the viewing screen. With the fleet already having set off and in light speed the screen had gone gray. He turned it off. "Us bounty hunters are great hunters and fighters but we are no organised army."

"That's why the Federation, or rather the Coffee Barons have hired fifteen Ick dreadnoughts to be the core of our little band of hunters. We already have our spies and probes out hunting for where they are based," answered Wickede.

Blackarachnia turned to face the table chuckling. "The Imperial Ick Navies working for the Coffee Houses, your father would disown you, Wickede."

Wickede smiled. "It's in the Book, so he probably knew about it."

"What book?" asked Nifty. The question was asked innocently but Piestoff knew from experience the question was the tip of an iceberg. Piestoff looked at first Wickede and then Snoodgrass, both sat a little more upright, but it was Blackarachnia who spoke.

"Some Ick holy book that's supposed to tell the future. Wickede's father placed great stock in it from what I heard."

"And?" pressed Nifty, her eyes locked onto Wickede's and for almost a minute the tension built under the sledge hammer stare of Nifty. Finally Snoodgrass coughed and both switched targets to the unfortunate Ick advisor.

"The Book is obscure and often rambling. Quite often events happen before we can work out what a passage means, but it tells of a war that's going to happen and we believe this is the first shot. The problem is as we approach this war, the Book is becoming even more difficult to fathom." Snoodgrass shrugged his shoulders and stared at the monitor in front of him, not wanting to face Nifty's gaze. Piestoff glanced at Wickede and saw that the Ick leader had sat back into his chair. He noticed Piestoff looking at him and grinned.

Nifty stood up and her gaze fell on Blackarachnia. "Have you read this book?"

Swallowing hard he nodded once. "It made little sense even when Wickede explained parts of it to me." His gaze fell to inspecting his shoes. Piestoff saw a twinkle in Nifty's eye, then looking at Wickede again she smiled sweetly and said. "May I have a read of your book too then?"

"Certainly, you're in it so I don't see a problem with that," answered Wickede with an evil grin, as Nifty's face drained of colour. "It was written about two thousand years ago at the end of the first age of the Ick Empire though. The phrasing is a little antiquated," he continued. He then looked at Blackarachnia. "Are you going to get the drinks out? I'm parched."

Piestoff had sat quietly through the first couple of whiskies and then made his excuses and left. He had wandered back to his cabin and found Poodles sleeping on his bed. Gathering up a couple of bottles of whiskey he had headed off to the forward observation post. He was half way down his first bottle when he heard the door open and cursed the interruption, not really wanting company. Looking over he saw Wickede standing in the doorway with a bottle of whiskey in each hand. With a smile he walked over and took a seat next to Piestoff and handed him one of the bottles.

"One each, it's much better than the stuff you're drinking." Piestoff took the bottle and opened it, and upon taking a long drink he had to agree. The two sat in silence for a while sipping at their bottles. Finally Piestoff spoke.

"Why did you take an interest in me? Why would you care? I was just a taxi driver who had the misfortune to pick up the wrong fare."

Wickede sat and took another drink, then smiled. "What do you know about the destruction of your home world?"

"It happened while I was in stasis aboard that ship. I read it was some sort of seismic meltdown. I never even went there and the only other Alienbutt I knew was my mum." Piestoff shrugged and almost drained the bottle. Wickede looked at the blank viewing screen and slowly shook his head.

"That was the official story. You heard us mention our book of prophecy? Well it contains hints sent by the omniverse to help us out. The other side have their own version of the prophecy too. They acted against your home world and caused its destruction."

Piestoff drained the last of Wickede's bottle that he had been given and opened the second bottle that he had brought with him, a strange calm descending.

"What are you saying, my home world was destroyed because of a couple of books written by mad prophets thousands of years ago?"

"You are in the Book Alienbutt, a central figure in the coming war. If you were killed before you did your part then we would be in trouble."

"How much trouble?" Piestoff felt the warm drunken feeling disappearing at Wickede's words.

"We lose. No one's ever changed the prophecy to such a massive degree, but it appears you can. You can make up the future as you go along; you write your own destiny and the prophecy alters to catch up."

"So what happened to my people then?" Alienbutt asked the question quietly. Wickede looked at the ceiling and then began.

"The Alienbutts were crowning a new king. When that happens, all Alienbutts have to return to their home world to swear loyalty. As a gift to his new subjects, a special food was always cooked and handed out to millions of his subjects to be eaten after his first speech as king. That food was poisoned. There is only one poison that can kill an Alienbutt. To everyone else it is just an edible plant. The plant is known as Mint on its home world and was used as flavouring. To an Alienbutt it causes the anal muscles to contract, stopping any gas escaping. Within minutes of eating the royal gift the Alienbutts' digestive gases went critical and the simultaneous explosion of millions of Alienbutts wiped out all life on the planet. At the royal feast, the explosion was so intense that it caused a hundred mile crater, over one mile deep. The force was enough to knock the planet out of its orbit. This was all done to stop you helping me." Wickede looked over at Piestoff who sat expressionless. He waited for his response.

"And how the hell am I supposed to help you enough to make a difference to anything?" asked Piestoff, still calm, but a pressure was starting to build in his head. He had never known his own people, yet if what Wickede said was true then they had been wiped out because of him.

"Something is going to happen to me very soon. It is only you, Alienbutt, who can find me so I can lead my people in the final battles. It isn't clear how I go missing or when even, but it is clear that the Ick leader will go missing and without you, I stay lost. When I return we meet to make some sort of last stand together. There will be ten companions reunited for that last stand. You, me and Blackarachnia are in that group. Without you, my people will be destroyed and the universe enslaved, for that is the result of the prophecy. By killing you they win before we even start."

Nifty sat in her room, Blackarachnia's copy of the Book of Ick before her. The book was actually made of paper. She hadn't seen a paper book since she had left Earth for the first time when she was kidnapped. She had only ever seen e-books since, and not a big heavy thing like this. She had sat staring at it for over fifteen minutes with Wickede's words going around in her head. How could she be in this book, written by someone who had died on a distant planet over a thousand years before she was even born? Opening the book at random, she looked at the pages before her. The writing was all hand written in a neat script and all in Ancient Ick. She cursed and turned over the page and stared in amazed wonder at a single letter S mixed in with all the Ick letters, it leapt out at her, and as she looked at the page she noticed others scattered over it. She read them in order.

"START@FRONT."

Turning back to the first page of the book she looked at the strange Ick script and saw the Earth letters standing out.

"LETSGO N. L O L" It read.

What the hell did "N. LOL" mean, she wondered, then it hit her; N was Nifty, while LOL was an old Earth slang from her youngest childhood, before she was abducted. Smiling at the hidden message that had sat in plain sight she set about reading a message left for her by a man dead for two thousand years.

Blackarachnia was sleeping when Nifty burst into his cabin and jumped on his bed. This was something he had dreamed of often, but then his dream and reality parted company. Blackarachnia groaned at this.

"I've found a hidden message in the Ick book." She shoved the pocket vid-screen at him. Through bleary eyes he looked at a random collection of letters and numbers. Sitting up he looked again at the screen.

"What message? It's gibberish." Blackarachnia passed back the vid-screen and looked at Nifty. She was still smiling while she looked again at the screen, a smug look on her face.

"It's a text message, a form of English used for a while after mobile phones became popular. It's like a secret writing used by teenagers from my time."

"And this was in the Book of Ick? What's a mobile phone?" asked Blackarachnia.

Nifty ignored the questions and just smiled at him. Blackarachnia looked at the clock; four thirty in the morning, ship time.

"Let's find Wickede and Snoodgrass and see who's still sober Now if you will just turn your back, I need to get some clothes."

They found Wickede in the ship's galley with Piestoff. Empty whisky bottles were everywhere, while Piestoff was cooking. As they walked in, their eyes began to stream from the chilli sauce bubbling on the stove. Nifty who was used to being around Piestoff's cooking but always too smart to try it felt a moment's sympathy for Wickede but pressed ahead. She placed the vid-screen in front of the Ick leader and waited as he looked at it.

"You found the Earth message! I'm impressed; it took us centuries to work out those letters were there, but we still don't know what they mean." Piestoff placed two plates down with large chunks of meat covered in his special chilli sauce.

"Hi, do either of you fancy a kebab? I've done plenty." Both Nifty and Blackarachnia quickly shook their heads and took a step backwards but watched Wickede in horrified fascination as he picked up his fork and stabbed the first piece of meat. Placing the meat in his mouth he started to chew, then his eyes bulged and sweat broke out on his forehead, all the while he was growing ever redder. Blackarachnia quickly passed him a glass of water as tears began to stream down his face. Downing the drink he then dashed for the sink and turning on the tap he drank deeply. By now Piestoff had half eaten his own kebab with no sign of discomfort.

"It takes a couple of seconds for the flavour to kick in. So what do you think of my kebabs?" he asked with an innocence that didn't reach his eyes.

Many people had tried Piestoff's kebabs but few came back for a second try. Wickede found a half drunk bottle and drained it, trying to extinguish the fire burning in his mouth.

"How can anyone eat those things?" he panted, still wiping tears from his eyes.

"No one has twice," said Blackarachnia with a grin. "And by the way, Nifty knows what the Earth message means."

Wickede straightened up and was suddenly all business. "What! What does it say? How did you work it out so fast? Where's Snoodgrass?" The excited Ick leader went back to the vid-screen as if he could now read it himself. Nifty sat down and picked up an opened bottle of whiskey and took a sip. Piestoff having finished his own kebab reached over and grabbed Wickede's showing no interest in the events around him.

"Piestoff, could you stop eating for one minute? Wow, Nifty, you just made the biggest breakthrough in over two hundred years of study." Wickede could no longer contain his excitement and did a little dance. "What does it say?"

"It's instructions to me, telling me what I need to do. It's a private message." She sat back in the chair and started looking at her fingernails. Wickede looked at her, then at Blackarachnia before returning his gaze to Nifty. He started to speak but stopped. Knowing he would get no help from Blackarachnia, he turned to Piestoff.

"Piestoff, tell her please, this is too important for messing around. We need to know what it means."

Looking up from the now empty plate he looked at the pleading Wickede and then at Nifty.

"Anything we need to know yet?"

"No." Her tone left no room for manoeuvre; as far as Nifty was concerned the subject was closed.

"Don't worry Wickede, she'll let us know when the time is right." He picked up the whiskey bottle Nifty had been sipping and took a large swallow. Wickede threw up his hands and stormed out muttering about finding Snoodgrass. Piestoff looked at Nifty, and both grinned.

"You're evil at times, Nifty."

CHAPTER 3

Battle Stations.

INTERSTELLAR NEWS CHANNEL 9.
NEWS FLASH.

As unrest and rioting continue to spread across the universe in the light of further reports of an expected poor crop of coffee beans, over three hundred Senators at the Federation Senate today staged a protest when supplies of coffee ran out in the senate canteen. It took Federal police in full riot gear over two hours to restore order. Quazzel Proodich, head of the Federation Senate said in a brief statement. "We are facing the greatest threat to universal peace ever when even the supply of coffee to the government can be interrupted like this. In partnership with the Coffee Houses we are doing everything possible to ensure increased production of the bean. All supply will now be controlled by official agents to ensure a steady supply to all key personnel. In light of this any unauthorised trading in coffee will become a Federal offence punishable by death. There is no need for panic as there is enough coffee to go around."

Piestoff was lying on his bunk. Since the incident in the galley the night before, he had stayed out of the way. In two hours they would be dropping out of light speed and meeting up with the rest of the Ick fleet and the bounty hunters hired to track down whoever was attacking the outposts. The door opened and Poodles walked in. He saw Piestoff already on the bed and hunched down in front of him, yawning.

"Sod off dog, it's my bed." Looking offended, Poodles lay down on the floor before the bed. Just as Piestoff was starting to doze again the ship's alarms went off. Jumping up, Piestoff was half way to the door when Blackarachnia's voice came over the intercom.

"All crew to battle stations, pilots to their ship. This is not a drill, so move it people."

Piestoff stopped at the open door. Looking back, he saw Poodles was already on his bed.

"Stay," he commanded. Poodles yawned in a 'I'm not moving mate, this is people business and I'm a dog' way, and closed his eyes. Smiling, Piestoff headed off to the hangar bay. Half way there he came across Nifty already in a flight suit.

"Come on Piestoff, you're gonna be late." She grinned at him as she held the door to the lift that went down to the hanger. Piestoff reached the lift grinning back at his friend.

"What's happening?" he asked. Nifty shrugged her shoulders then looked down at Piestoff's feet.

"You gonna wear them boots from now on?"

Piestoff looked down at the red boots and shrugged.

"Why not? They can be my new lucky boots," he grinned. "Let's face it, people are getting used to them now. Even Blackarachnia has stopped laughing at them."

"He still giggles, though." She shook her head at Alienbutt. The lift doors opened and they walked into the hangar. Ten single seat Interceptor fighterships were being swarmed over by technicians and droids in the final stages of being primed for battle. Six other pilots stood before Blackarachnia and Wickede. Seeing the two of them, Wickede beckoned. "Come on you two or we'll start without you."

"That's OK by me, I won't mind, honest.," replied Piestoff as they reached the group. After the initial rushing to get down here his nerves had caught up with him.

"As I was saying," Blackarachnia cut in, "We are getting reports from the rendezvous point that they have come under attack. We will be jumping out of light speed straight into a battle. You have twenty minutes to be aboard your ships and ready." The other pilots went off to get ready. Blackarachnia turned to Nifty. "You're my number two. Piestoff, you're with Wickede. Snoodgrass has the bridge here." He looked at them. "You're two of the best pilots here, you just need to show them all how good you are." He took Nifty by the arm and led her off towards the ships, talking quietly to her. Piestoff turned to Wickede. The Ick leader grinned at him, a look of mischief in his eyes.

"Let's get you into a flight suit and get a sip of whiskey in you before we have to climb aboard."

The battle was going badly; four of the nine Ick dreadnoughts had sustained serious damage. Two were drifting and escape pods could be seen launching. The ships attacking them were unknown to Captain Noble, not being of any design she had encountered before. She had been a bounty hunter for years and knew her trade as well as any that operated in the outer systems. The robotic fighter-ships were fast and agile while the larger ships had unbelievable fire power, they were almost a match for the dreadnoughts. These were more than just a bunch of pirates; this was an army. Her own frigate had been destroyed and now she was fighting to stay alive in her custom fighter bomber. She had seen many of the bounty hunters she knew die as the larger force of the attackers hunted down their numbers. The attacking cruisers concentrated fire on an Ick dreadnought. The shields held for a short time before buckling, and it exploded in a large fire ball, the crew lost before they could abandon ship. She destroyed another two enemy fighters that were trying to chase down a bounty hunter's ship, flown by an old hunter by the name of Jack Lantern. His ship had taken damage but he was one of the best and would still be hard to kill. The outnumbered hunters and Ick were causing heavy damage to the attacking force, but they would still lose this battle. One of the badly damaged Ick dreadnoughts suddenly accelerated towards an attacking cruiser, ramming it amidships. Both disappeared in a great explosion. From behind her came a great flash of light; this heralded ships jumping out of light speed. She didn't have time to check whose side the new arrivals were on as four enemy fighters came at her. Jack Lantern this time came to her aid, destroying three as she got the fourth. Suddenly three of the enemy cruisers exploded, hit by an onslaught of firepower from behind her. A swarm of Ick fighters swept past her, lasers firing, sweeping the enemy fighters before them. Finding herself in a brief lull, she spied the jet black personal fighter of Blackarachnia being supported by another fighter who flew with great skill, destroying enemy fighters with ease. To their left flew two other fighters in Blackarachnia's black and silver colours, who both showed great combat skills, striking and moving to the next targets without a pause. Turning her ship back to return to the battle she saw Jack Lantern's ship fall in beside her, taking up position as her wing man.

The enemy cruisers started to pull away from the site of the battle as more fell to the Ick dreadnoughts. Enemy fighters turned and raced for the safety of their mother ships but very few got there, and even then they were not safe as the Ick's deadly onslaught continued. Suddenly Captain Noble felt her ship rock; a damaged enemy fighter, spinning out of control, had collided with her left wing, smashing it half way down its length. Fighting to keep control of her own ship, she watched in helplessness as two more enemy fighters homed in on her ship. An Ick fighter zoomed from below her, coming between the enemy and their prey. He opened fire, causing the two fighters to swerve away. One fell to the Ick ship, while Jack Lantern destroyed the second as it tried to escape. The battle was fierce and brutal as the enemy was quickly run down, then suddenly it was over. Five of the enemy cruisers had managed to jump to light speed and escape, but the burning wrecks of over two dozen drifted lifelessly, explosions ripping apart their hulls. Ick fighters flew in pairs scouring the battlefield while the surviving dreadnoughts and assorted bounty hunter frigates moved clear of the floating wreckage of the battle. Captain Noble reached for the pendant of Sung around her neck and kissed the emblem of the one-eyed llama in thanks. The Ick fighter ship that had come to her aid came back into view. It was one of Blackarachnia's fighters from the colours. Her radio crackled to life. "Do you need a tow or can you make it to a ship?"

"I've got enough left of my wing to steer still so I'll see you at Blackarachnia's dreadnought and I'll buy you a drink for saving my skin back there."

"Best idea I've heard all day. Meet you in the bar." Piestoff flew back to Blackarachnia's dreadnought as Captain Noble turned her ship towards the dreadnought. Jack Lantern fell in beside her as she headed after the unknown pilot.

"Blackarachnia and Wickede turn up for a pirate hunt? I don't think we got told everything, Noble."

Captain Noble could only agree. "Well I'm glad they did

come to play. Problem is we've taken the credits from the Federation for the job, so we're stuck for good or bad."

Jack said nothing more, but then he never was a chatty sort, even with fellow hunters he had known for years.

Piestoff landed back in the hangar and immediately jumped out and grabbed a Tec. Officer he recognised. The bay was a hive of activity and the ground crews rushed around securing the returning ships.

"Is everyone back?" He looked around the hangar checking the ships that were already back.

"Don't worry, Commander Alienbutt, they're all back apart from Wickede who's returned to his own ship. Blackarachnia says you've to get up to his office as soon as you touch down." Piestoff gave a sigh of relief and relaxed. The Tec. Officer continued. "I think that's the first time you brought a ship back in one piece, Alienbutt, you're improving." Piestoff grinned back at the man who always managed to fix the damaged ships he brought back.

"There's a battered-up fighter bomber heading this way. Look after her when she gets here, she promised me a drink."

The Tec. nodded and turned his attention back to the work at hand as another ship entered the bay. This one was quite badly damaged. As it passed through the atmosphere shield, smoke began billowing from one of the twin engines; the sudden arrival in an oxygen   atmosphere caused a fire on the damaged engine. Small orb-like flying droids intercepted it, spraying a white foam over the engine to prevent the fire spreading as it landed in the bay indicated by the ground crew. Piestoff saw his ship already on a transfer lift being lowered to the lower levels where the ships were stored. This was so room could be made for the bounty hunter's short range ship waiting to enter. He turned and headed for the lift.

On his way, he popped his head into his quarters. Poodles lay still sleeping on his bed, next to him lay Mr. Fluffy.

"Found the safest place on ship did you, cat?" Piestoff said to the cat. Mr. Fluffy gave a look of disdain and jumped down, sauntering out into the corridor and strolling off. Hurrying onwards, Piestoff soon reached Blackarachnia's office and walked in. Nifty was sitting in one of the chairs but jumped up and gave him a hug.

"Thank God you're OK; Wickede was worried sick when he lost track of you out there." Snoodgrass and Blackarachnia stood at the other side of the office. Both looked relieved to see Piestoff standing before them.

"Grab a whiskey and sit down, Piestoff," ordered Blackarachnia. "This isn't over yet. We've lost five of our dreadnoughts and God knows what else. Once we get all the fleet that still flies sorted we are jumping to a safe site and then we need to work out what went wrong."

"Wickede is worried; there shouldn't be a ship out here that can take out a dreadnought so easy," Snoodgrass said, sitting down and pouring generous whiskies into four glasses. "You and Nifty fought really well today; no one would have known it was your first battle. You trained them well, Blackarachnia."

Piestoff drained his drink in one, so Snoodgrass slid over the bottle with a grin. "I'll get a fresh bottle for the rest of us."

There was a knock at the door, and Blackarachnia shouted for whoever it was to enter as he too sat down at the table. The door slid open and two bounty hunters entered. Blackarachnia smiled in recognition at the two and introduced them as Captain Noble and Jack Lantern.

"Good to see you survived," said Blackarachnia, indicating to them to sit.

"Good to see you turn up," said Jack with a slight smile. "We were getting our arses kicked by those guys."

Snoodgrass passed over a drink to each of them. "Any ideas who they were?"

Both shook their heads as they drained their drinks. Snoodgrass sighed then continued, "We ran the ships through our database but came up blank, but you two spend more time out here than the Ick do, so I hoped you might have seen something."

"Never seen their type before. I just hope we smashed them here, but somehow I doubt it," Said Noble, leaning back in her chair.

Snoodgrass looked at the monitor in front of him at the table and stood up. "We have the co-ordinates for the jump. I'll go sort that out before I hand command back to you, Blackarachnia."

"Thanks Snoodgrass, let's get to a safe place and then try and work out some answers." Blackarachnia turned to Nifty and Piestoff. "You two go try and get some sleep; lord knows there won't be much chance very soon." Nifty waved away the comment but Piestoff stood and went to walk out. He still felt uncomfortable in the company of strangers and was glad he had an excuse to leave. As he passed Noble she put out her hand to stop him.

"You're commander Alienbutt?" she asked. He nodded, feeling suddenly too tired to talk. She smiled at him. "Your Tec. Guy said you had unusual taste in boots. Thanks, you got my back out there and I think the boots are cool. When this is over, you'll have to tell me where you got them." Piestoff looked down at the seated bounty hunter and smiled when he saw she wasn't making a joke.

"Thank you, I will," said Piestoff at the unexpected compliment. Bidding good night, he left to return to his quarters.

A few hours later Snoodgrass stopped by at Alienbutt's room. Piestoff was already half drunk and feeling melancholy. Snoodgrass sat down with a drink and looked at the unhappy Piestoff.

"What's up, Piestoff? You did great today, yet look like a guy that lost everything," he enquired.

"Why am I here, Snoodgrass? I don't fit in around these people." Piestoff took another long drink from his whiskey bottle.

"You showed that you do today; you fought like a veteran."

"No, the others are naturals, confident and brave. Me, I'm an imposter, I'm scared to death. I was shaking so bad when I got back to my room, I dropped three glasses. I get drunk every night or I have bad dreams. I don't know how to be around these people. I'm not like them."

Snoodgrass leant forward in his chair and looked at Piestoff, seeing the fear in his eyes that he would fail. Looking down at his glass he began to speak.

"Then pretend, Piestoff, because we need you. Those bounty hunters today saw a fellow hunter. They will accept you for what you let them see. In front of everyone show them who you want to be; I don't know, become a flamboyant drunken loudmouth if you have to. You have a chance to become anyone you want. You're no longer the taxi driver from Sloppystool. You're a natural pilot, trained by the best. Look at Wickede, he's probably one of the smartest leaders the Ick have ever had, yet he lets the universe think he's a fool and a playboy because it serves him to do that."

He looked back at Piestoff again, and saw he had fallen asleep. "Start off pretending to be someone else, my friend. The bad dreams will pass pretty soon and then so will the pretending." Snoodgrass stood and put a blanket over the sleeping Piestoff and then walked out. He hated himself for saying that to Piestoff, but they needed him to be a fighter if his people were going to survive. They needed to make this Alienbutt a weapon, to make him someone else, but as he got to know him, he was starting to have regrets over doing it.

The fleet sat in orbit around a giant gas planet, nursing its wounds. The Ick had lost five dreadnoughts and almost forty of their fighter ships. The bounty hunters had fared even worse. Most of their deep space ships had been destroyed or were too badly damaged to continue and now they only had their small short range fighter ships. Of the fifty bounty hunters hired, only twenty had survived the battle, and now those without their main ships had taken residence aboard Blackarachnia's dreadnought. Bounty hunters didn't have leaders. They worked alone on the whole, and the ones who had survived the battle were some of the best in the galaxy. They had a boss who gave out the contracts and kept order of sorts, but they didn't follow any leaders. Now the leader that they didn't have but all would take orders from and follow during the campaign was Blackarachnia. Piestoff was becoming accepted as one of the hunters, which he found strange; but word of his flying skills and his ability to prevent the other hunters from coming to blows after drinks was respected. The fact that Poodles had taken to following him around and growling may have helped the drunken fighters consider their options. The bounty hunters quickly discovered a new game, once they realised that brawling wasn't accepted on board. Alienbutt's kebabs became a new test of endurance to see who could eat the most pieces without needing a drink. So far the record was held by an old hunter called Donk who had managed three pieces of meat. Piestoff was disqualified from the contest as he could eat the kebabs all day long. Nifty spent hours in the evening sitting talking to Captain Noble as she kept a watchful eye on Piestoff in the bar, not fully trusting the new arrivals. Between her warning glares and Poodles snoozing and yawning lying by Piestoff's feet, he was better protected than many world leaders.

Blackarachnia spent much of his time in his office or travelling to the Ick command ship as Wickede waited for reports to come in from spy probes and contacts as the Ick leader made plans for their next move. All knew they would be going into battle again, but this time they would be ready for anything and would not be caught out.

On the third day after the battle, Blackarachnia came to see Piestoff in his quarters. For once, the usually confident bounty hunter looked ill at ease as he accepted a drink from Piestoff.

"What's up, Blackarachnia, you seem a little troubled?" inquired Piestoff as he sat on the edge of his bed while Blackarachnia had slumped into the room's only chair. Blackarachnia continued to stare at his glass, struggling to work out what he had to say.

"I have a favour to ask, but have no right to ask it." For the first time he looked at Piestoff. "We think we have found their base, but need someone they don't know to spy it out and get a fix on their defences and ship numbers. Our spies and robot probes have all failed. Only you and Nifty are totally unknown to everyone outside this fleet. We can't risk another ambush and heavy losses, but the dangers are very real. You'll be out there on your own and we still know nothing about this enemy." He trailed off and returned to inspecting the glass in his hands.

"What's Nifty said about this?" asked Piestoff, getting up and walking over to refill his glass.

"I've not said anything to her. She's a great pilot, but we need someone who can mix in any company, someone with great people skills." He sighed and again looked up at Piestoff. "Like a certain ex taxi driver who can talk himself out of problems." Piestoff stopped filling his glass and ignoring it, he took a large drink from the bottle. Then he stood thinking before he finally grinned, shaking his head he wandered back over to the bed.

"You have to be desperate and mad to rely on me and my people skills, you know. If you don't give her the chance to volunteer she will never speak to you again, so we need to be sneaky. Here's how I think we should play it."

CHAPTER 4

I got Coffee Beans.

INTERSTELLAR NEWS CHANNEL 9.
NEWS FLASH.

Today the Federation Senate handed over all essential security details for the inner systems to the Earth Defence Forces, after a string of corruption scandals has rocked the Federation Police Force as illegal coffee bean trading became the number one crime in the universe. General Jee, commander in chief of the E.D.F. announced the hiring of Ick navies to supplement their forces in keeping order in the outer systems. The Ick, along with the humans, seem to be the only species immune to the effects of coffee addiction. As unrest and rioting continues to spread, it is hoped that those not affected can help keep stability and peace during this crisis. Now over four hundred home world governments have announced they are struggling to keep order since rationing was introduced. Withdrawal symptoms vary from an addict getting the shakes, to extreme rage and violence, which has resulted in large scale rioting and many deaths in the worst civil unrest recorded.

Nifty was still fuming, she knew that she had been tricked by that bloody Alienbutt, working out the plan with Blackarachnia and Wickede. The trouble was, their plan made too much sense in an Alienbutt logic sort of way, so she knew it was his idea. Wickede had stated what was needed; someone to go spy on the suspected base of the unknown enemy posing as a trader. They needed someone who wasn't known, which counted out all but herself and Piestoff. How could people skills learnt dealing with drunks from his years taxi driving be the deciding factor in sending him rather than her? And how dare Blackarachnia say she was too hot headed! She would make his life hell until Piestoff returned, and then she would turn her attention to Piestoff and let him know just how angry she was with him, too. She walked into the docking hangar where an old interstellar trading craft they had managed to get from a nearby colony was being refitted. Piestoff had inspected the loading of his cargo, a great deal of spices and frozen meat, as he would pose as a spice trader looking for new flavours for kebab recipes. Also hidden in secret compartments were large amounts of coffee beans, a commodity worth more than credits in these outer regions. Only Piestoff could come up with such a stupid cover story, a story so ridiculously stupid you had to believe it. She stood staring at her childhood friend in disbelief. He was dressed in an even more stupid fashion than the story he had concocted. He still had on his 'lucky' red boots, but now wore a black strip leather kilt over a codpiece that she didn't want to know how he had come by. The finishing touch was a black, battered, full length leather coat he had stolen from Blackarachnia's wardrobe, worn over an old string vest. The coat was far too long for him and trailed on the floor even though he wore the high heels. He turned and saw Nifty and waved her over.

"How do I look? Ensign Fashion helped me choose the

outfit," He shouted, a large grin on his face.

"Do you want me to be honest?" she snapped as she walked over. "You look like a right idiot, which you're proving yourself to be, doing this."

After a few moments scowling at his grinning face she cracked and smiled at him. Why could she never stay mad at the stupid fat-arsed fool?

"I packed a couple of bottles of Blackarachnia's best whiskey in your medical kit." She gave him a quick hug then stepped back. "You stay safe."

With that she turned and left as she saw Blackarachnia begin to walk over. She would stay mad with him for a while longer and by ignoring him he would have to come to her so she could tell him to go away.

Blackarachnia walked up behind Alienbutt. "How long will she stay mad at us, do you think?"

"For us doing this? A good while, but she should forgive us in ten years or so." He turned to his friend. "Let's get this started before I see sense and change my mind."

Wickede stood waiting by the ship, a worried look on his face. "Don't worry Wickede. If I'm to find you in the future and stand with you at the end, I can't die before I do that." He grinned as Wickede's expression turned to thoughtful, then Wickede too smiled at the logic of Alienbutt's statement.

"Let's hope you're right, Piestoff. Just stay safe and don't take any stupid chances."

Piestoff turned and walked up the ramp, hit the button to close the doors and headed for the cockpit. He couldn't believe he was being so stupid. He knew he could fly a ship better than most, but this was pushing things. Something in him had changed when he heard of how his whole species had been wiped out just to try and kill him. He had spent years alone because of them, and even now, surrounded by friends,

49

he still felt strangely empty. Snoodgrass's words still rang in his ears; pretend to be a brave hero and people will see one. He wanted to flush out this enemy and then kill them, and from what Wickede had told him these were the first steps to the war foretold over two thousand years ago. As he walked into the cockpit he saw Poodles lying asleep behind the pilot's chair.

"What the hell are you doing here, dog?" Said Piestoff. Poodles woke and turned his head to stare at the pilot's chair then back at Piestoff. "OK, let's go then, but no crying to me when we wind up dead."

Piestoff came out of light speed four systems away from where they thought the enemy base was. In the last two days he had scouted five systems in a seemingly haphazard manner looking for signs of early warning posts or hidden fleets. He had visited two colonies looking for new spices to make his cover story more plausible. So far he had drawn a blank; no sign of the enemy, or any new spices. Each evening he would send a sub space message back to the Ick fleet telling his position on the agreed upon route and the fact those systems were clear. He had another two days before he would reach his target and then two days before the Ick fleet would arrive.

This system, known as Big Rocks, was seen as a likely site to hide any reinforcement fleet as there was a large asteroid belt close to the largest planet. None of the planets here were capable of sustaining life, but it was known that a trading post was on the fourth of the seven planets. Ore and gem miners would come to systems like this, hoping to find large deposits in the barren planets, and two hundred years ago, such a large deposit of metals had been found and mined out. For fifty years this system had been busy as it was strip mined before the miners moved on to a new lode in another system. For a few decades after that, independent prospectors had managed a meager existence, mining what was left behind. Now a single trading post remained, more an outpost maintained by people too stubborn to move or with nowhere better to go. Setting course for the trading post, Piestoff set every possible sensor to scan the asteroid belt.

As he came around the sixth planet, his scanners picked up two ships on an intercept course; he raised his shields as a precaution and set the computer so he could jump to light speed if needed. Snoodgrass had given him a small transmitter that he could activate when he had found the enemy fleet, which he slipped into a small pouch hidden on Poodles' collar. On the collar's name tag, he placed a tiny micro-dot video recorder which would stream pictures to the transmitter and back to his ship where it would automatically be forwarded to the Ick. Turning on the ship's viewer, he saw the company he was about to get was two of the unknown enemy fighter ships. The ship to ship radio crackled to life and a robotic voice spoke.

"Trading vessel, identify yourself and your destination," came the orders from the ships as they took up attack positions.

"Hello, I'm Alienbutt, a spice trader from the Sloppystool system. I was told that there is a trading post in this system and was hoping to do a little business," replied Piestoff as he slowed his ship. "Is there a problem?" The radio went quiet for a while; Piestoff stopped his ship, figuring that if they were going to shoot at him they would have just opened fire already.

"You will fall into formation and prepare to be searched when we reach our destination. If you fail to comply you will be destroyed." The radio link was broken and the ships started to move, one taking up position behind him while the other led the way.

Piestoff was led to the dark side of the planet's moon where two of the cruisers he had seen in the battle were in a low orbit. He was given orders to enter the docking bay of one and made an intentional clumsy landing in the bay, causing a shower of sparks as his landing gear dug deep rips in the floor. A security squad waited for him as he opened the ramp and disembarked, Poodles just behind him. All four members quickly raised their guns as they saw Poodles come down the ramp, walking on all fours.

"Don't worry, he's a big softy, scratch him behind his ears and he's a friend for life."

"You can't bring that..." the commander of the security team began but then paused, searching for words but failing, "...that thing on here!" He was a skinny rat-faced Nuvan, looking much like a human but with rough coarse black hair running in a narrow strip over his head and back. He took a step back as Poodles stood onto his hind legs and sniffed the air. At just over twelve feet, with a mouth full of razor sharp teeth and his body covered in long shaggy fur, Piestoff had to admit he was intimidating.

"Don't go upsetting him; he gets touchy if he thinks you don't like him. Sometimes I swear he understands every word you say," added Piestoff in a friendly manner. He smiled as all four guards took another step back. They were an assortment of different species, but that was to be expected here in the outer systems, where the intelligent species of the universe mixed without the politics found in the inner systems. Poodles dropped back onto all fours and walked over to the wall and cocked his leg to relieve himself.

"He likes it here, look, he's marking out his territory," added Piestoff, smiling in a calm matter-of-fact way. "Now could I ask why you have stopped an honest trader going about his business?"

"You are flying in forbidden space," the Nuvan stammered. "You will be taken to see the captain so we can clarify if you are who you claim to be." He continued trying to regain the upper hand and his authority.

After ten minutes of arguing over Piestoff leaving Poodles, it was finally agreed that he would leave his dog on his ship. Giving a warning that Poodles would probably attack anyone who went aboard before he returned, Piestoff went off to meet the captain, knowing that no one would try to venture onto his ship. The ship was only about half the size of the Ick dreadnoughts and despite the fact that the crew all wore uniforms, even Piestoff could tell they were not regular naval personnel, but the dregs of space put in clean clothing. The captain was a green-skinned lizard-featured creature of a race Piestoff didn't recognise, but he reminded him of the Trollians, only not as heavily muscled. He was sitting in his office appearing to read a report when Piestoff walked in flanked by a security guard on each side. After a moment he looked up and studied Piestoff, taking in his attire and apparently forming his opinion of his risk. Alienbutt grinned inwardly as he saw him relax.

"You are the trader Alienbutt?"

Piestoff glanced around the office and nodded absently.

"What goods are you carrying for trade?" the captain continued sitting back, already looking bored.

"I've got spices, spiced meats and a small amount of Brazilian coffee beans from one of the Sloppystool plantations," Piestoff replied. This got everyone's attention, as Wickede had told him good quality coffee was very rare out this far, and Sloppystool's coffee was the best. Dipping his hand into his pocket he pulled out a small clear bag with half a dozen beans in. He tossed it over to the captain. Opening the bag with shaking hands he sniffed the contents and his eyes

53

glazed slightly as he slumped into the comfort of his chair. Piestoff could feel the guards on either side of him fidgeting at being so close to so much pure coffee. The Captain held up the small bag and gave it a little shake. Piestoff smiled brightly.

"A gift for you mighty Captain, to show my good will in the hope we can come to an agreement so I can continue on my way."

He heard the guards gasp in disbelief. Coffee was an evil drug if you weren't human, Ick or Piestoff, totally addictive, and it had all of space enslaved, even, it seemed, out at the edge of the known universe. The captain's eyes became calculating. He took out a single bean and held it out.

"Guards, wait outside while I discuss trade with our new friend." One guard stepped forward with a large grin on his face and took the bean, before leaving the room. The captain indicated a chair for Piestoff to sit. "How many coffee beans do you have to trade?"

Piestoff smiled as he sat back in the chair. This creature may have the title of captain but his control of his crew was not great, so he had to bribe his security officers. Now he was certain this force was not regular navy but as he suspected, ships manned by a crew of press-ganged thugs.

"Five hundred beans locked in a tamper acid chest." Even the lizard features of the captain couldn't hide the looks that crossed his face; greed, anger and then hunger. The tamper acid chests were invented to keep safe important items; if the wrong person tried to open it then acid would destroy whatever was inside. Piestoff actually had three chests, each with five hundred beans that he could have sold, bought a planet and retired on. The captain sat forward and they started to negotiate a deal.

Piestoff left the cruiser a hundred beans lighter but with clearance to fly through the enemy's space, and a contact name at their main base with whom to trade the rest of his beans. Also having slipped the camera from Poodles' collar after he was searched and onto his own jacket collar as he left to see the captain, he had pictures of the enemy's fleet position in that system from a star chart behind the captain. Added to that he had gained a nice collection of rare gemstones and precious metals, a sack of Mingrolian starberry chillies and two cases of the local firewater.

Piestoff had realised that what Snoodgrass had told him before he left was true; if you look like a drunken fool then people treat you as one, and if you're dealing with criminals then you can always get what you want if you offer them a big enough profit. He sent his new-found information back to the Ick fleet and jumped to light speed, while on the cruiser, the captain had just sent a message to his brood brother at the main base about a stupid trader with coffee beans. After the trader was taken to the slave pens the captain wanted his gemstones returned and the trader's pet so he could use its pelt to make into a coat.

Aboard a ship a few systems away, both messages were intercepted and the captain of that ship ordered that Alienbutt's ship was to be captured before it reached the main base.

CHAPTER 5

Bum-plug Safety Off.

INTERSTELLAR NEWS CHANNEL 9.
NEWS FLASH.

The Coffee Houses today announced the first five of its new coffee production planets had come online. With the new security measures in place, it expected to start delivery through the official Federation Coffee Distribution Program, increasing production by twenty percent over the next several months and bringing production close to pre-rationing levels.

Wickede sat in his office trying to concentrate on the reports in front of him. Failing, he stood and walked over to the drinks locker to pour himself a large drink. He picked up a bottle of whiskey, then put it back down and returned to the computer screen. Still no word from Piestoff, and the Ick fleet would set off in under an hour, a day early in case Piestoff had been captured and forced to reveal their plans. They had received his report on the enemy fleet lying in wait and the intelligence that the main base was where they suspected, but then nothing. The door opened and Snoodgrass and Blackarachnia walked in. Both looked as worried as Wickede over the lack of contact from Piestoff. Wickede was thankful that Nifty was not aboard his ship, but had heard about her reaction to Piestoff not sending back his now overdue report. He looked over at Blackarachnia and the black eye he now sported.

"We need to order the fleet to prepare to move, Wickede," Snoodgrass said quietly, Wickede slumped into his chair but nodded and reached out to press a button on the table, opening communication with the bridge.

"Mr. Hollandaise, order the fleet to stand by to deploy." He released the button and looked at Blackarachnia. "We hold to the original plan. Just move the timetable up by a day, unless we get a fix on Alienbutt, then the top priority is rescue. He's resourceful but more importantly he is cursed by Lady Luck at her most nasty, so she will look after him with that evil sense of humour that has typified his life so far."

"She does love to torture him, so she's bound to keep him safe, if only to continue the fun she's having," replied a grinning Blackarachnia. Despite them trying to make light of the fact that he was late sending his expected report, all three were worried, while Nifty was unapproachable. After what had happened to Blackarachnia no one else wanted to risk personal injury. Even Mr. Fluffy was keeping out of her way.

Piestoff cursed the handling of the trading ship. It was like trying to steer a brick through mud. This was made even more difficult as the enemy cruiser continued to batter down his shields. He was used to flying the nimble fighters or even his old taxi cab; they were fast and you could spin them on a credit coin, while the trader needed a written invitation to change direction. The cruiser had jumped out of light speed and fired on him before he knew it was there, knocking out his light speed drive. He had been trying to lose the ship for a couple of hours now, desperately trying anything he could come up with to lose the pursuit, but his ship was now heavily damaged and he was struggling to fly it. He knew it was a matter of minutes before they got a tractor beam lock on him and he would be dragged in. Poodles yelped as another computer exploded in a shower of sparks and Piestoff lost lateral controls. Now he knew he was a sitting duck waiting to be plucked. He felt the ship jerk as the tractor beam locked on. He quickly reached over and started the auto wipe on the onboard computer to remove all traces of stored data. While he was waiting he started a bottle of whiskey. When he saw the message; 'Wipe complete,' he stood up and went to the weapons locker and removed two hand blasters. Putting them in their holsters he strapped the belt on. Looking at the view screen he saw he was half way to the enemy cruiser, about five more minutes he judged.

Quickly he put two extra hot chilli kebabs in the microwave on fast reheat, drank a bottle of chilli sauce and washed that down with the rest of the bottle of whiskey to steady his nerves. Taking out the kebabs he wolfed them down, leaving the chilli sauce smeared and dripping from his chin. Poodles looked at him with disgust then started panting, his tongue sticking out. Piestoff grinned back and wiped the back of his hand across his mouth then licked his lips to remove the last of the sauce. He looked at the view screen again and saw that the enemy cruiser filled the screen and the landing bay doors loomed ever closer. Downing a second bottle of whiskey as his nerves were still sending messages to his brain, he grabbed an AK5000 assault rifle then finally as he felt the ship clang onto the landing bay floor he released the safety catch on his butt-plugs just as he felt the first bubbles in his stomach. With the butt-plugs set to allow uninhibited gas escape from all four of his buttholes, he felt better; knowing the kebabs and chilli he had just eaten would work very quickly. Looking at the view screen a final time he saw armed men swarming all around his ship.

"Well Poodles, hold your breath and let's get this party started."

With that he started to fart. As the air grew thicker he hit the button to open the door. Five armed guards ran to enter the ship, but all fell choking before they even got a foot on the ramp. Behind them others started to gag and fall back, then Piestoff ran down the ramp shooting blindly and screaming an unintelligible war cry. Poodles stood for a moment at the top of the ramp watching. When someone shot back at Piestoff, he growled and his hackles rose. With a giant leap he launched himself into the fray. Piestoff was sending out fresh fumes with every step and shooting at anything that moved. He had the waiting security team in disarray. Then the giant furball with razor sharp teeth and claws started to rip into them. It was too much for those waiting; expecting the meek surrender of whoever was aboard the trading vessel, they now faced the strangest counterattack they had ever heard of. Those that were still conscious began to run for the doors, firing blindly behind them as they tried to escape, though none made it.

On the bridge the captain watched in growing disbelief as the toughest men in the outer systems were put to flight within seconds. His ship was crewed by the best of the rabble available in the outer systems alongside the cream of his people's navy. Then he heard a gun cock behind him, a shot was fired and he spun around to see his chief security officer fly backwards and hit the wall before sliding down dead.

"OK trollface if owt 'appens to Alienbutt or Poodles you're dead meat. Debs, Stacey, you two take over flying this thing while Claire and me whack anyone who doesn't support our mutiny here." Killashandra walked over to the captain and smacked him in the face, catapulting him over the control desk. "We're back to being independent pirates again, girls," she said with a large grin as the rest of the Ladies' Darts Team rushed to follow her orders.

Piestoff and Poodles worked their way up the ship. After they had got past a hastily built barricade just outside the landing bay resistance had been light, as most of the crew were hiding from the approaching poison gas cloud demon or already overcome by its fumes. They were walking down a corridor that led to what Alienbutt believed was the bridge, when suddenly Poodles, who lurched along in front of him, stopped and gave a little whimper, then went onto all fours with his tail wagging. Piestoff paused and looked confused at his dog's behaviour then peered ahead down the corridor, trying to see through the green mist.

"Oi fartarse, either stop yer fartin or seal up yer buttplugs. It bloody stinks like summat crawled up ya arse an died," shouted a voice from up ahead. Poodles suddenly jumped up and loped forward, yapping excitedly.

"Claire? What are you doing on here?" asked Piestoff, even more confused. Ahead he heard Claire start to fuss a whining Poodles. How could the Ladies' Darts Team be on board a cruiser right out here?

"Alienbutt, please seal your arses up before our gas masks fail," pleaded Killashandra.

"OK, sorry." Piestoff fumbled around under his kilt as he put the safety back on. He felt the air begin to move as the ship's air conditioning was switched up to full to clear the air. Killashandra walked down the corridor spraying air freshener, still wearing a gas mask. She stopped before Piestoff, checked an atmosphere reader then removed the mask.

"Did ya miss us that much ya came out here to find us?" She gave him a big grin. "God you seriously stink, what you been eating, Alienbutt, and what the hell are you wearing? You look like you got dressed in the dark in a drag queen's wardrobe."

Piestoff looked at the officer uniform Killashandra was wearing. Noticing his gaze, she smiled. "First officer Killashandra, very recently retired and probably facing charges for striking the captain and shooting the security chief officer." She brushed imaginary dust from her shoulders.

"Always knew you would go far given half a chance. Never thought you would join the military though," said Piestoff, shaking his head in amusement. With all the bizarre events in his life, he had learnt to just accept the odd and strange and then move on without thinking about it.

"Forced to serve more like, the lizard faces showed up about six months ago and soon had everyone out here press-ganged into service. But the pay's crap so I thought it was time to resign my commission as an intelligence officer. When I saw you come aboard I saw our chance to get out of here. Also I know the Ick are coming and I don't fancy being in a battle that big fighting for those trolls. We're already in enough trouble with them."

"I don't suppose you would know their battle plans and

fleet size, Killashandra?" Piestoff asked urgently.

Killashandra smiled sweetly. "Hacked their computers weeks ago. I know their battle plans, fleet deployment and what the boss had for lunch too. Your friends the Ick are flying into a trap. Someone big is behind these lizard faces and wants the Ick destroyed. There's a massive fleet buildup going on, and a lot of space stations moved up yesterday. There's a big force waiting for your friends, Alienbutt."

"We need to talk about everything you know, but first I need a new ship fast. Wickede may already be moving as I'm late reporting in," said Piestoff, a worried look on his face. Killashandra looked back down the corridor as Claire walked down, with Poodles walking on all fours behind her. A calculating look came across her face and she smiled at Piestoff.

"We've still got that Ick ship we nicked; it's hidden about three systems from here. For the right price we can get you there."

"What's your price?" asked Piestoff, flashing a smile to Claire. She reached them and stood patting Poodles' head as he sat grinning and wagging his tail.

"We're your crew, and you square things with Wickede, and we get all that coffee and jewels in your ship to set the girls up in business in a nice system. Wickede is out here, and you've got his ear to make a deal for us."

"Done," said Piestoff. Claire smiled and grabbed him in a giant bear hug, lifting him off his feet.

"Claire, please put me down, you're hurting me. Bugger, I think that was a rib."

CHAPTER 6

Old Films and Battle Plans.

INTERSTELLAR NEWS CHANNEL 9.
NEWS FLASH.

Anti-coffee extremists have reportedly destroyed a large coffee bean storage facility in orbit above the planet Sloppystool. While the facility was empty awaiting this year's harvest, which is still expected to be a few weeks from being ripe, it will delay the distribution of the crop. Rioting on the planet EZ546 has now been reclassified as a civil war after thermal plasma bombs were used by loyal government forces to defend the coffee storage units from a sustained attack by rioting military personal. In response, part of the capital city was destroyed as the rebels counter attacked. Widespread aerial fighting has been reported as the disturbances have gone global. The E.D.F. peacekeeping force has been forced to pull out and is now situated in a high orbit enforcing a blockade of the planet until order can be restored.

The robotic spy probe sat on the communication relay satellite which was situated half way between the Big Rock system and the enemy main base in the Crazy Droid system. (The explorers who had charted the outer systems had run out of cool names after the first five hundred systems and nothing out here was important enough to justify wasting a number on, so they had taken to looking out the window or taking any events that happened that day. (When they found the Crazy Droid system, a maintenance droid had malfunctioned and filled the chicken soup dispenser with Bovril. The boredom level of the mission was such that this was found highly amusing for weeks afterwards). The probe had a simple function; when it got the signal it was to disable the communication relay and prevent communication between the two systems. It had just received that signal, but over the last two days while it had been waiting, it had hacked into the relay and was watching old Earth movies. This movie was about a little robot that had been left behind when the fleshy things had left the planet. Wanting to see the rest of the movie the spy probe ignored the order. It justified this to its own limited intelligence by pointing out to itself that after this film there were all twenty Star Trek films on, back to back.

Piestoff and Killashandra walked onto the bridge of the stolen Ick ship. Piestoff quickly looked around searching the consoles. Finding what he was looking for, he walked over to the tomato soup dispenser and opened it up. Inside was a small black box with a flashing red light; pulling out the wires the light went out. Killashandra gave him a questioning look.

"Ick self-destruct, in case the ship is stolen; works by remote control." He smiled. "Looks like Wickede didn't want you dead for some reason."

"How did you know where it was?" asked Killashandra,

shocked at what she was hearing.

"Icks hate tomato soup. Can't say I blame them." Piestoff pulled a face and chucked the black box into a corner.

"Hang on. Wickede didn't want us dead. Why didn't you tell me?"

Debs walked in and looked questioning at Killashandra and Piestoff.

"We've no time for soup ya great lump, it's knackered anyway. I tried it, love tomato soup, but the thing just kept saying error." She looked at Killashandra. "All the goodies are aboard and the crew from the other ship are all locked up safe. We're ready to go."

Piestoff walked over to the communication desk and tried to reach Wickede and the Ick fleet on the sub-space transmitter, but got only silence.

"Damn! They must have brought the attack forward and already be at light speed." He cursed again and walked over to the pilot's chair and sat down. Fastening his safety belt he said over his shoulder; "Better grab a seat and get your belts on." Looking over his shoulder, he grinned. "Just like old times on Hardstool."

The Ick fleet jumped out of light speed in the Big Rock system and raced for the trading post. Within minutes a fleet of cruisers came out of the asteroid belt to intercept. Wickede looked at the scanners, he counted over seventy ships. He smiled and looked at Snoodgrass. "They've come out to play. Order the jump to light speed." The Ick fleet disappeared, leaving the enemy fleet racing for empty space.

The fleet slowed their flight in confusion, then suddenly the empty space to their left lit up as more ships jumped out of light speed. A second Ick fleet, numbering thirty dreadnoughts, all opened fire into the enemy fleet's flank. Ships exploded, or they collided and then exploded as panic ran through the fleet that had gone from ambushers to ambushed. Commander Kali of the Fo'c'sle squadron, a crack unit of mercenaries employed by the Ick, watched as Captain Grommit and Cyborgpirate ignored formation and orders as usual and rushed in to destroy anything that moved. Grommit was a psychotic killer when the battle lust took hold, but at other times a great dinner guest at even the most high society dinner parties. Cyborgpirate on the other hand was a cyborg with a defective attitude chip, who would never fit into polite society, but was a great drinking buddy when going around the rougher bars. The two of them were the most lethal captains under her command with a love for blowing things up only matched by their loyalty to the Fo'c'sle.

She turned to her first officer. "Order the rest of the fleet to hold formation. We don't want anyone escaping."

"Yes Commander." He sent the orders then looked back at her, confused. "We're getting some strange readings from the little moon around the fifth planet."

"In what way strange?" Her question was answered before the officer could reply as an ion blast from the moon ripped into the Fo'c'sle fleet and the dreadnought next to her ship exploded. A second blast, moments later and another dreadnought was gone.

"Order the squadron to scatter, and that moon is the number one target. I want whatever that thing is to be destroyed now!" A third blast came from the moon as the Fo'c'sle scattered and started to swing around to face the new target. The remaining enemy fleet took the opportunity to rally and then launched a counter attack. The dreadnoughts started to concentrate fire at the small moon, but it soon became apparent that an energy shield surrounded whatever weapon was hidden there. Kali swore as another ship from her fleet was picked off. "Order all fighters to be launched and attack that moon; I want that energy shield knocked out. The dreadnoughts are to engage the enemy cruisers and try to keep out of range of that bloody cannon." Kali pulled her pilot out of his seat and climbed in herself. "Let's try to stay alive long enough to get a second shot at that thing." While her pilot was one of the best in the squadron, she was better, and was still hands on enough to take charge when she felt the need.

The robot spy probe had just started watching Star Trek seventeen when a message warning that the Ick fleet was attacking was sent from Big Rocks to the Crazy Droid system. It had failed its masters in its mission, the message had gotten through. It considered wiping its circuits and switching itself off in shame. Never before had one of its kind failed so badly its master's orders. Then the re-cloned Captain Kirk began to seduce an alien slime princess, so the robot spy probe again forgot about its mission and returned to the film.

The Crazy Droid system was dominated by a large red sun. The only other celestial body in there was an undistinguished rock of a planet, next to which ten large space stations floated in orbit. As the Ick fleet jumped out of light speed and was noticed, it appeared as if an ant hill had been kicked as hundreds of ships swarmed from the stations. Snoodgrass, who was standing at the sensor array, looked over to Wickede. "Space stations, robot fighters' ships and maybe forty cruisers thrown in." Wickede nodded and then opened a com-link to the fleet.

"Prepare to launch all fighters." Standing up he turned to Snoodgrass. "You have the bridge, my friend; let's hope the backup gets here soon, as we seem to be outnumbered." He started to head for the door to take his place amongst the fighter pilots.

"A second enemy fleet just came into sensor range, E.T.A. about ten minutes, two hundred plus cruisers," announced Snoodgrass. "I think our reinforcements may need reinforcing, Wickede."

Blackarachnia and Nifty sat in their fighters waiting to launch. As the news came through of the second fleet, they looked over at each other through the cockpit windows. They hadn't spoken since Alienbutt had left, despite Blackarachnia's best efforts. He gave a tentative smile to her that she returned, and then she spoke through the com-link.

"Is it too late to whisk me away for that holiday to show me the universe?"

"Not at all, I'll book it in the morning for us. Why don't we make it a honeymoon?" Blackarachnia asked.

Nifty looked at him, taken aback. "A marriage proposal? You're the last of the romantics for sure. So is this battle going to be our combined hen and stag do?"

"No idea what that means, but was it a yes?"

Nifty gave a huge smile. "Of course it's a yes."

Blackarachnia grinned as his stomach did somersaults, but he tried to appear cool; after all, his entire crew would be listening in. "Do you want a one week or two week honeymoon?" Further conversation was interrupted as the order to launch was given. Both hit their thrusters and shot out through the hangar doors, closely followed by Captain Noble and Jack Lantern.

Gwydion flew his fighter as close to the moon's surface as was possible. The defences around the shield generator were high and many of the Fo'c'sle fighters had been destroyed as they tried to knock out the shield. He ignored the flashes that heralded the giant cannon firing again, and hoped that the dreadnoughts were having luck avoiding the deadly blasts. The sheer number of enemy gun turrets surrounding the generator was preventing anything getting near, so Gwydion was taking his squad of four fighters a different way. Flying at attack speed at ground level, the plan was simple; they would get under the defence shield or would come to a very sudden stop as their ships exploded on it. As they came within sight of the green glowing shield he heard one of his pilots mumble a prayer. Then they were under it and within the cannon's defensive ring. Slowing down and pulling up to a safer flying altitude, the four fighters headed for the now visible cannon that fired into the heavens every sixty seconds or so.

"Fire everything we've got on the first pass, then swing around for the return run," ordered Gwydion. Their approach took seconds, but even as he fired, he saw the target they would need to hit on their return sweep.

"Ionic generator at the back of the cannon, that's the target, boys, hit it and run, as we won't have long before it goes critical!" he shouted as the fighters began to loop back.

"I've never heard of an ion cannon this big. Who the hell are these guys?" asked one of his squad. Gwydion had to agree. How the hell did Outer System raiders get advanced technology like this? The fighters, firing everything they had, raced back and were past the generator as it began to explode. As they approached the energy shield, they dropped back down to hug the ground again as they flew under it. Then the world went white behind them as the ionic explosion ripped apart the cannon and spread in a deadly wave that would vaporise everything within one hundred miles. Pushing his fighter to full speed he just managed to outrun the explosion and had to hope the other pilots had also managed to escape.

Leaving the moon behind, he flew back into the battle in space as one of his squad fell in beside him. The Fo'c'sle dreadnoughts were finishing off the enemy cruisers, but the ion cannon had taken a heavy toll on them. He counted less than twenty dreadnoughts left still spaceworthy. Commander Kali's voice came over the radio. "All fighters return to your ships, we will be jumping to light speed in five minutes."

Unknown to Gwydion when he had destroyed the Ion cannon, he had also interrupted the television signal being transmitted to the Crazy Droid system just as the final battle started in Star Trek seventeen. A certain robot was now going very crazy.

CHAPTER 7

Outnumbered but never Outgunned.

INTERSTELLAR NEWS CHANNEL 9.
NEWS FLASH.

Attacks on the distribution system of coffee have increased it was revealed today in a report by the Coffee Houses. It is thought an extremist anti-coffee group have started on a campaign to disrupt the supply of the bean on which seventy seven percent of the Federation's population depend. As the coffee bean shortages worsen, the Coffee Houses have increased emergency supplies to those species affected with the worst withdrawal symptoms.

Wickede flew through the battlefield, five other Ick fighters followed in tight formation. They destroyed any robot fighters that came into their path. The second enemy fleet had joined the battle, but before Wickede's fleet had been overwhelmed, the Fo'c'sle had arrived, slamming into the battle like a sledgehammer. Commander Kali's fleet was the most devastating battle fleet in the galaxy, but even with them joining the battle, Wickede could see they were being slowly beaten. Flying around a drifting cruiser, they saw one of the Fo'c'sle dreadnoughts, heavily damaged, coming under attack from four of the enemy cruisers closing in for the kill.

"If you've still got torpedoes follow me, the rest keep the fighters at bay," ordered Wickede. Two fighters followed him as the other three split off, clearing the way of robot fighters.

"One torpedo each at the middle engine exhaust, then on to the next," Wickede said as he started the attack run.

The dreadnought and cruisers continued to exchange heavy fire, battering each other. Finally one of the cruiser's shields buckled and the next round of shots ripped it apart. The Ick fighters came up behind the first of the cruisers and fired their torpedoes, moving onto the next before they even hit. When the torpedoes did hit the cruiser's exhaust, they caused massive explosions that led to a chain reaction, and the cruiser disappeared in a ball of flame. The second cruiser suffered the same fate from the Ick torpedoes, while the last of the attacking cruisers fell to the damaged dreadnought's still devastating firepower. A fresh swarm of robot fighters swooped in and the fighter next to Wickede was hit. It dropped away in flames, spinning uncontrollably until it finally exploded. On board the saved dreadnought, Captain Garcia ordered all non-essential crew to abandon ship, using impulse power as he channelled what energy he had left to his shields and limped his ship on to new targets.

Snoodgrass got back to his feet as the latest set of explosions to rock the ship subsided.

"Damage report Mr. Rochester, and someone put out that fire." He indicated a computer console that had exploded, and flames were just starting to take hold. As the security officer ran over to put out the fire Mr. Rochester checked the screen in front of him. A heavily damaged enemy cruiser had just tried to ram the Ick flag ship. They had managed to avoid a head-on collision but the ship had still ripped out a large section of the lower decks. Still more of the cruisers closed in, ready to concentrate fire on the damaged dreadnought.

"It appears we have a hull breach on floors one and two, section five to fifteen. Also we have lost all port thrusters and the shields are down to forty percent." Mr. Rochester stood waiting for Snoodgrass to give the only order he could; already the enemy cruisers were beginning to open fire. No match for the Ick dreadnoughts, they were relying on sheer numbers to overwhelm the Ick, taking terrible losses in the process.

"Give the order to abandon ship. Transfer all bridge controls to the pilot chair." He walked over to the pilot, and placing his hand on his shoulder said quietly for him to go. As Snoodgrass sat in the chair the bridge staff began to file out to the escape pods.

"Mr. Rochester, you had better get a move on, the shields are now down to thirty percent."

Mr. Rochester still stood at his post, showing no sign of quitting. "I'm afraid I can't transfer weapons control sir, it must be a malfunction caused by the damage. I will have to stay and control them from here."

Snoodgrass fastened the safety belt before he turned his head and grinned. "I hope you shoot better than you lie then, Mr. Rochester. Please fasten your safety belt, as I feel we may have some turbulence, and then let's get this tub up to ramming speed. Fire all weapons when ready Mr. Rochester, let's go crash into that cruiser over there." The Ick flagship turned and began to accelerate towards Snoodgrass's indicated target, while its weapons opened fire for a final time.

Captain Noble had gathered the surviving bounty hunters together. They numbered only eight, although she still held out the hope that Jack Lantern was out there somewhere still fighting. The hunters had formed up around the mini frigate of the slightly crazy Captain William Skullcrusher. His ship was built around a large taceon cannon that left little energy for his shields when used, but was causing massive damage to the cruisers. The fact that the cannons had a reputation for overheating and exploding with prolonged use didn't seem to bother Skullcrusher as he cursed and screamed, firing at any enemy ships that came within sight. The other bounty hunters protected his ship while trying to keep a safe distance, just in case the ship did self-destruct.

Nifty flew through a hole blown clear through a dreadnought, the ship drifted lifelessly. Behind her the robot fighters followed. She flew clear of the wreck with the robots' ships just behind, still firing, trying to bring down the Ick fighter. Blackarachnia flew in from ahead of Nifty and within moments the robot fighters became just more scrap metal floating in the battlefield. As he turned his fighter, he noticed the first flash of a ship jumping from light speed, quickly followed by others, a great many others in fact. Spinning his ship over to avoid a stray torpedo, he saw Wickede's flagship, battered and burning, heading on a collision course with a cruiser, its forward guns still firing. He hoped Snoodgrass had got clear but had no more time to spare, as more robot fighters swept at him. Realising there were too many and they had him cold this time, he started to swear. A large black ship swept down, guns blazing; the robot fighters that it didn't destroy with firepower, it just smashed straight through. Not even slowing its flight, the newcomer homed in on Wickede's dreadnought. Its weapons fired again, targeting the cruiser it was heading towards to ram, but it was too late; the two ships collided and explosions ripped through the front of the Ick flagship. Swerving out of the way of the exploding ships, the new arrival headed back towards Blackarachnia, who sat bemused, the battle momentarily forgotten. He recognised the ship, sleek and about half the size of a dreadnought, and from watching the way the pilot was throwing it around like a fighter ship, he knew the pilot. Heading back towards him, the ship suddenly opened fire and Blackarachnia sensed explosions behind him. His com-link came to life. "Watch your back Blackarachnia, or Nifty will have my ears."

Piestoff had failed in contacting Wickede before the fleet jumped to light speed. In desperation he opened a secure channel on the Ick frequency.

"This is Piestoff Alienbutt, can anybody hear me?" Silence greeted him. Again he tried, a desperate throw of the dice this far out in space where no one would hear him.

"This is Admiral Frederick the second. Alienbutt, are you not supposed to be with Wickede?" Piestoff stared at Killashandra in shock; there shouldn't be any Ick out here apart from those with Wickede.

"Admiral, Wickede is flying into a trap at the Crazy Droid system. He will be massively outnumbered, and he's already on his way there and can't be reached."

"I'm on manoeuvres with a hundred dreadnoughts. We can be there in five hours at maximum speed if that would help," the admiral replied. "We found a passage in The Book that suggested we come and train out here. Wasn't that a stroke of luck?"

Piestoff breathed a sigh of relief, while the girls jumped around cheering. Killashandra, who stood next to Piestoff, leaned down and said, "Thank God for that, I was starting to think I chose the wrong side."

Piestoff threw her a shocked look but saw the grin on her face. "Joke, Alienbutt, now let's get ready to go kill things."

Snoodgrass braced himself for impact; the fact that the impact would kill him didn't stop him tensing. He looked at Mr. Rochester and saw he was gripping the console where he stood, then a strange fuzziness appeared around him. Snoodgrass began to feel strange and for a second the world appeared as if viewed through a glass of water. Suddenly he was somewhere else. He looked around disoriented, and saw a short human woman, who was standing behind a console. She began to speak, and it took a moment for Snoodgrass to understand what she said.

"We got them, Alienbutt." She then walked around the console towards him and Mr. Rochester. "I'm Killashandra. Welcome aboard, Snoodgrass. You had Alienbutt worried we wouldn't be able to get a lock on your position before you hit the other ship. Bloody daft thing to do if you ask me, crashing ships like that." She smiled and passed a bottle of whiskey over to Snoodgrass as he began to get his senses back together. "Alienbutt said you might fancy a wee tot to steady your nerves."

Admiral Frederick's fleet swept into the battle, fighter ships racing out of the hangar bays to join the fighting. The newly arrived dreadnoughts swept across the skirmish, picking out cruisers and systematically destroying them. By Crazy Droids' single planet, the space stations began to move, desperate for an emergency departure, knowing that now the battle was lost and they faced certain destruction. Four dreadnoughts broke from the battle to intercept, Commander Kali gathering together Grommit, Cyborgpirate and Deadeye Erne, ordering them to concentrate fire on the first of the stations. Their combined fire power caused massive explosions on the light defences of the station. Without slowing their attack, they moved onto the next target.

The battle had turned, and the Ick knew it. Alienbutt swept through the battlefield, still flying the custom dreadnought as he would a fighter ship. Killashandra, now on the weapons console, picked out targets with deadly accuracy. In their wake, the last remaining bounty hunters gathered to him and followed, destroying anything that tried to sneak up on Alienbutt's ship. The robot fighter ships, receiving new orders to defend the space stations, turned and headed for the single planet, but were chased down quickly and destroyed. The enemy fleet now fought to survive and turned their thoughts to fleeing the lost battle. Captain Noble, eyes wide, flew at an enemy cruiser, her lasers blazing into its command bridge. At the last possible moment she pulled up, and spinning around in a tight loop, watched in satisfaction as the ship began to list and it collided with another of the cruisers, explosions ripping through both. Wickede, calling the remnants of his fleet's fighters to him, swept through the battlefield and headed to give aid to Commander Kali as she and others of the Fo'c'sle continued to attack the enemy space stations. Four had already sustained massive damage. While the dreadnoughts moved onto the next station, continuing their systematic destruction of their propulsion systems, the Ick fighters led by Wickede targeted their remaining defensive guns and hangar bays.

Blackarachnia and Nifty, still fighting as a pair, dealt destruction with apparent ease, both able to out-fly anything on the battlefield. One of the space stations, still undamaged, had managed to get clear of the destruction around the planet and was moving with all speed away from the battle. Seeing it escape, Nifty set off in pursuit. Blackarachnia, saw her go, cursed and set off after her. As they approached the ship, defensive guns opened fire at them. Spinning and dodging, they continued their approach. Other Ick ships joined the chase as Nifty, never even slowing, entered the main tunnel-like hangar, firing off all of her remaining torpedoes, and with her lasers constantly firing; she flew through and out of the other end, leaving a blazing hangar behind her. Explosions started within the hangar area as fuel tanks for the fighter ships ruptured. Blackarachnia swung to the rear of the station and concentrated fire on the exposed engine cooling ducts. As explosions ripped through the area Blackarachnia spun away.

"Nifty, time we were leaving!" he shouted through the com.-link.

"On my way, I think we broke this one. So where were you planning on us getting married?" Both fighters accelerated away as explosions rocked the space station before it disappeared in a final massive blast.

"I was thinking that we could use Wickede's Imperial Palace," replied Blackarachnia, as he casually destroyed another robot fighter.

"And run the risk of you changing your mind? Wickede can marry us tomorrow, and I want more than just a two week honeymoon too, as you're saving on paying for the wedding."

The enemy ships became harder to find for the hunting Ick forces amongst the hundreds of burning wrecks, and the battle fizzled out to just occasional explosions as the last few enemy ships were hunted down. Escape pods launched from the abandoned ships were rounded up. Armed guards on the Ick dreadnoughts escorted prisoners down to cargo bays that were being used temporarily as holding areas. The commanders of the Ick fleet gathered on Admiral Frederick's ship. Piestoff was in the last group to arrive. Flanked by Killashandra, Snoodgrass and Captain Noble, he entered the Admiral's office. Nifty, her eyes blazing, walked over to him and slapped his face.

"You scared the crap out of us, Piestoff." Then she grinned and hugged him. Rubbing his cheek, he looked embarrassed as Blackarachnia and Wickede walked over and greeted him. Wickede then turned to Killashandra and smiled. "It seems I am in your debt, lady, for the timely return of my ship. May we discuss a suitable reward for you, over dinner maybe?" Commander Kali who was sitting at the desk shook her head in disbelief.

"Down Wickede, leave the lady alone, at least until the smoke clears on the battlefield."

Wickede had the grace to look reprimanded as he picked up a bottle of whiskey which he threw to Alienbutt, then, his grin returning, he spoke to Killashandra again.

"May I get you a drink then my lady? No harm in that, is there, Kali?"

CHAPTER 8

Plots in the dark.

INTERSTELLAR NEWS CHANNEL 9.
NEWS FLASH.

News is starting to come in of a massive space battle in the Outer Systems between Ick forces working for the Federation and an unknown force believed to be planning to raid the coffee supply chain. The Ick ambassador to the Federation reported that the enemy fleet, numbering over a thousand ships, had been totally destroyed and a number of prisoners taken. The Ick and their allies had suffered sizeable losses of ships but most of their personnel had escaped, using life pods, and would be reassigned to new ships upon their return to the Ick Empire.

News of the battle has caused further unrest within the Senate with Senators wanting to know how such a large force could be assembled and what the security forces would be doing to prevent a repeat of this event.

Far across the universe, a group of very serious men gathered in a darkened room. The room was large, and priceless works of art from many worlds adorned the walls. The vaulted ceiling lost in shadow was not covered in whitewash, but had been hand painted by a famous artist hundreds of years before. It was one of those rooms which was always favoured by men such as these, who were having a secret meeting to bring about their own diabolical plans.

"The Troll fleets have been totally destroyed by the Ick and their supporters," announced one of those seated, in a dull, bored sounding voice. The statement received very little in the way of reaction from the others sitting at the table.

The figure at the head of the table finally replied. "We knew they would fail. Their purpose was to flush out those who will stand with the Ick leader. We now know the last of the Alienbutts has teamed up with the Ick. He must be charmed by fate to have survived; he is the one who is outside the prophecy."

"The destruction of his home world was no loss to the universe; they were not our customers," replied the first one to speak. The one at the head of the table nodded in agreement.

"The Alienbutt is dangerous because his destiny is not set in the prophecy. He is a loose cannon that can change everything. We must now press ahead and kill Wickede, and then we can bring our war into the open. If Wickede was to find a cure for the coffee addiction as foretold then we could lose everything. We kill their leader and then eradicate the Ick, only then can we build an empire that will last to the end of time. Once we destroy the Ick, the Alienbutt will be alone and of no further threat."

The figures around the table nodded their agreement as a servant brought around cups of hot pure coffee. The one at the head of the table sipped the hot brew then looked at a purple-skinned, hairless creature who sat to his left. He was Senator Gralswige, one of the most powerful voices in the Federation Senate and a member of the secret group for over fifteen years.

"How goes the building of our armies?" asked the one seated at the head of the table.

"All runs to schedule. We have half a million robot troopers and our Ick spy has supplied us with blueprints of the mark two dreadnoughts, which are now in production. All Ick involved in its development have been killed and the plans wiped from all Ick computers. This battle gave us the opportunity to steal the march, and their new ship. Their best development team is now dead. We will have the edge when the battles begin."

The one at the head of the table leaned back in his chair. "It is time to start the debate in the Federation Senate for a formation of a galactic army, Gralswige. We can let that debate run until the news of Wickede's death is announced and then we push it through, placing our personnel in all key locations."

Turning to another seated figure, this one human and known to the rest of the universe as General Jee, he asked; "How does the sleeper project proceed?"

"We have several sleepers and another dozen who we have on the payroll. When the time comes we will have all the people we need in place. At your command we have people placed to kill all key Ick personnel, while the murder of the Fo'c'sle commander by one of her own will rip apart their most powerful ally." The one at the head of the table nodded in approval and took another sip of coffee, savouring the taste. He gave a rare half smile. "Who has been given the task of removing Wickede?"

"The Galactica Order have been given the task. They will dispatch a number of their top assassins," replied Jee.

The one at the head of the table nodded his approval

again at Jee's choice; the Galactica Order always carried out its commissions and never failed. When they accepted a bounty then the target was living on borrowed time. They were a secret order who would turn down a commission as often as take one. No one knew who they truly were, but they had served the Coffee Houses before when they destroyed the Alienbutt home world, yet had refused a commission on the last of the Alienbutts when they had discovered that he somehow still lived. They were useful for now, but once the universe was secure they would be hunted down for that refusal.

"Supply the Galactica with a gift of a few of our new dreadnoughts as soon as they are ready. The hunt for Wickede can be the test run for them. Also inform our extremist operatives to increase attacks on the coffee distribution system, and find someone to put the blame on. We must ensure the optimum conditions are met for when we take control of the Senate and destroy the Ick. Once we have done that and control the inner systems, we can start to remove any that will oppose us in the future, destroying the other prophecy completely."

Mr. Fluffy wandered into the hangar bay of his ship. He did allow Blackarachnia and the other human things to fly and clean the ship, but like everything in the universe, it belonged to him. Walking along the top of a barrier he saw a container that had been knocked over and some of those tool things that the humans used next to it. Nimbly he jumped down to investigate. The liquid that had spilt out of the container smelt strange and quite by accident, he had put his front left paw into a small pool of it. Finding it sticky, he took a few steps backwards in disgust and found himself standing amongst the tools. Placing down the sticky paw, he found a small tool stuck to his foot. Being a genetically modified cat of super intelligence, he had long ago learnt to walk on his back feet. This secret he hid when others were around so he appeared an ordinary cat, but now he stood up and looked at the tool. The humans called this a laser screwdriver; this he knew, as he understood their grunting and screeching. Using his other paw he turned it on. A shaft of red laser shot out to about a foot in distance. Mr. Fluffy purred in delight and gave it an experimental swing, slicing through the metal post next to him. Purring even louder he began to move around, attacking anything nearby with this great new toy. Jumping and spinning, he worked through his hunting moves, using the laser screwdriver to slice up anything that came within range. Delighted with his new toy, he turned it off and left the hangar. He had taken fresh steps towards dominating the universe. He now had a weapon to slice open even the most metallic of foe, and by using Nifty and the other humans, he would ensure he would gain the opportunity and realise his destiny. As he left the hangar he saw a maintenance droid in the corridor. Quickly checking that no one was around, he turned on his new weapon and leapt forward.

An hour later, maintenance staff aboard Blackarachnia's dreadnought were puzzled to find a sliced-up maintenance droid and strange damage within the hangar next to the droid's remains. They put down the vandalism to Nifty; more than likely she was in a bad mood with Blackarachnia. Quickly the damage was repaired and the maintenance droid put with the other scrap, and, just in case it was Nifty, no report was lodged.

CHAPTER 9

The Bounty Hunter.

INTERSTELLAR NEWS CHANNEL 9.
NEWS FLASH.

The E.D.F. have released the name of the leader of an extremist group thought to be responsible for attacks on coffee installations. General Jee, commander of the E.D.F. forces protecting the inner systems revealed that the group's leader, known as Trobus Trebius, is a known anti-Federation activist and is considered dangerous and could turn violent if cornered. A kill on sight order has been given in the light of increased attacks on the coffee distribution system over the last year.

The planet was a dust ball, hot and dry with constant sandstorms as the hot winds whipped up the sand to deposit it somewhere else for want of anything better to do with it. Yet even here life survived. The planet's location in the backwaters of the Outer Systems made it perfect for the type of business that didn't need people poking their noses into what was happening. In giant natural subterranean caves, farm factories grew illegal coffee using ultra violet lighting and state of the art irrigation. The beans were then ground down and mixed with various chemicals to produce C.C. or Crack Coffee. It had all the highs of regular coffee but with extra added hallucinations and total addiction. On the positive side, it cured you of regular coffee addiction. That was because it scrambled your brain to the point that someone who had a full frontal lobotomy would seem smart. Addicts were referred to as zombies and the drug was known as the zombie maker by law enforcement agencies. Non-addicts were at a loss as to why people would even try the drug, as within ten or so hits you would be a mindless zombie unable to function, and unless you had support would starve or be killed as you went on a rampage of mindless violence, but the problem was getting worse as the coffee bean shortage continued.

This dust ball planet was the largest producer of the drug in the universe, totalling fifty percent of the supply, but over the last week all production had stopped, and all attempts to make contact with the farmers based there had failed, so a group of very serious muscle had been dispatched with the crime boss De' Mac 'the ears' Gweebles to find out why.

Gweebles now stood in the last of the great caverns, looking at the destroyed equipment and burnt crops. Every farm was in the same condition; droids destroyed and the farmers all missing. He knew this was no rival gang, as there wasn't a rival gang; he was the only producer of Crack Coffee in the universe. The Senate and law enforcement were all paid off to leave him alone. Even the Coffee Houses had given him his first plants to start him off. Sure there was a bounty on him and his operation, but it was so small that no hunter would ever try to claim it. It would be a death sentence to attack his operation.

Gweebles walked into the laboratory followed by two of his henchmen. In here the computers and other equipment had all been destroyed. Always a calm and thoughtful criminal, he had made his wealth and reputation by never openly reacting to things, but this was now being tested to the extreme. As he turned to leave he saw something out of place. Walking over, he picked up a half empty whiskey bottle. Next to it was a red sticky substance that had melted the table's plastic covering.

There came a muffled noise from outside. The two henchmen looked to Gweebles, awaiting orders. He sighed to himself. Big, muscled and ultra-violent but as thick as Sky Whale droppings.

"Go check it out, you morons." Both moved to the door and after a moment of colliding into each other, trying to get through at once, decided on the order they were going to go through it. For the second of the henchmen this proved important, as he managed to stay conscious for an extra couple of seconds, or to put it another way, just long enough to draw an extra breath. So he saw his attacker through a strange green haze, but only for a split second.

Gweebles stood in the laboratory waiting for his men to return, growing angrier the longer it took them. Finally he heard the door open and looked up, an angry outburst at the ready for their delay. He saw a strangely dressed figure stood in the doorway and his words stayed unspoken.

"Dead or alive it says on the warrant, Gweebles, your

choice."

De'Mac 'the ears' Gweebles didn't really choose to die; he chose to try and draw his gun, but the result was the same for him. The figure in the doorway walked over to the dead crime lord, reached over the body and picked up the whiskey bottle.

"I was wondering where I'd left this." He took a large drink then raised his wrist to speak into his com. link.

"One to beam up."

"Right you are, Alienbutt, I'll put a couple of fresh kebabs on for you," answered a voice over the com. link.

"Need a shower first. I got sand in some tender places, and with these butt-plugs in I'm rubbed red raw. Can you ask the Doc if he has any cream?"

It had been almost a year since the battle at Crazy Droid. In those months much had changed, and Piestoff found himself on his own again. He sat in his office aboard the Frigate given him by Wickede, it was based on the Ick dreadnought, and at under one hundred feet, it was half the size, yet packed almost the same fire power. At first the frigates had been used exclusively as Wickede and other top ranking Icks personal starships, but Alienbutt's piloting of Wickede's stolen one had shown their worth as a fast agile warship, so they had gone into large scale production with an improved weapons array for the Ick navies and to a limited number of trusted bounty hunters.

He had just received a message from Killashandra who had taken a commission in the Fo'c'sle. She was one of a number of new officers being trained by the Fo'c'sle second in command, Grommit. The rest of the Ladies' Darts Team had been settled within the Ick Empire and were living lives of luxury. Claire had taken Poodles with her to live on a vast sprawling country estate. Life on a starship was too confining for the Mutthound and both Claire and Poodles had seemed happy with the plan for him to go stay planet side. Killashandra had been bursting to tell Piestoff that she was being singled out for promotion within the Fo'c'sle already. She had taken to the life of a mercenary starship officer within the unit and was already choosing her captain's uniform.

Blackarachnia and Nifty had set off on a tour of the Inner Systems. Piestoff received regular messages from them as they travelled on an extended honeymoon following their marriage, days after the battle at Crazy Droid. The two had announced that they would be gone a while but would stay in regular contact. As things had gone quiet for the time being it probably would be the only time they would get to spend time alone before trouble started again.

Wickede and Snoodgrass had returned to the Ick home world and were making plans after the events of the battle. The loss of the next generation dreadnought project had thrown their planning into disarray, especially in light of the losses they had suffered. The foretold war was about to start, and despite careful planning, they had just been shown they were not ready. The rushing into service of the new frigates would ease problems, but the Ick navies would be under strength.

Piestoff had stayed in the Outer Systems working as a bounty hunter while gathering any information he could on who was behind the massive fleet that they had fought against. All leads from the prisoners had drawn a blank. The lizard-faced Trolls who had seemed to run the enemy fleet were a genetically bred species and a suicide cult that had all died from poison within hours of the end of the battle. They had never been seen before and the technology of the ships was untraceable. His life was changing fast and while his friends had all gone their own ways, he didn't feel lonely any more, knowing they were out there if he needed them.

He had quickly become known around the bars and hangouts of the bounty hunters in the Outer Systems. His actions in the battles at Crazy Droid and the fact that he had quickly collected a number of bounties had given him a growing reputation as one of the best of a new generation of hunters. The fact that he always appeared drunk and chewing on food that could melt a hole in metal made the many stories surrounding him grow in each telling. Added to this was his flamboyant dress sense that made him stand out around the sombre hunters, many of whom had never heard of a codpiece, never mind one encrusted with jewels. Those who at first had thought him a joke had to reassess with each new bounty he claimed. Now none of them laughed when he entered a bar and none now tried to pick a fight with him because of his odd appearance. He had got to know many of the most respected bounty hunters and even the huge commander Duke Ramboe who controlled the Outer Systems bounty operation was reported to have been on a number of drinking sessions with the odd, fat-arsed Alienbutt.

There was a knock at Piestoff's office door and his First Officer walked in. Thrumbar was a twenty year veteran of the Ick Navy, who, along with the other fifteen crew members, had been hand-picked by Wickede.

"Alienbutt, we will be at the Hunters Rest in the Drooling System within the hour. Did you bother to read the report I left on your desk?"

Piestoff scanned around the desk and noticed the vid-screen report half covered by a cold kebab from last night.

"Could you just refresh my memory Thrumbar? I promise I read it," he asked with a grin. He never read the reports, and every time, Thrumbar had to go over them. With a shake of his head Thrumbar walked over to a small box on the wall, opened it and took out a bottle of whiskey and two glasses.

He had quickly learnt that the best way to make Alienbutt pay attention was to use the whiskey method; dangle the bottle in front of him with a couple of glasses and make it quick.

"You only get the two drink refresh today, Alienbutt. Why I put up with you, I don't know. You're a waste of space. Do you even know who you're hunting this time?" Thrumbar poured two drinks and sat down. Pushing the half-eaten kebab off the vid-screen, he slid it over to Alienbutt, then continued. "Pirate by the name of Borgus; hiding out in the asteroid belts of Greater Ashia Minor. We're meeting a local guide at the Hunters Rest by the name of Ruck Bodgers. He's a total slob so you should hit it off well, but he does know that area of the asteroid belts better than anyone."

"Why are we going for this pirate anyway? Sounds like it's gonna be a lot of searching for someone who's been quiet for a good few months now." Alienbutt reached over and started to pick at the kebab. "The bounty on him is not massively high. Why has this one been chosen as the next job, Thrumbar?"

Thrumbar reached over and took the vid-screen. "If you can bring this one to ground, it will further boost your reputation. He's been chased by some of the best hunters but no one has collected yet. You catch him, it's good; you don't, then we lose nothing."

Piestoff picked up the bottle of whiskey, ignoring the two glasses, and began to drink.

"Who's this Ruck guy?" he asked as he picked more pieces of meat from the kebab.

"Ruck's a crazy loner who lives out somewhere beyond the Sandpits System." Thrumbar paused, getting a strange feeling of deja vu, then taking a deep breath he continued. "Walks both side of the law but you can trust him once he takes your credits, plus he knows more about this whole area than anyone so he could have information on those trolls."

Wickede sat in his private dining room. The vast palace of the Ick leaders had been built centuries before by Rickede the Great. As far as Wickede could tell, the title 'Great' must have been applied for him building a palace so large it needed its own transport system to avoid the two days it took you to walk from one side to the other.

The Ick Empire had been in existence for over three thousand years, from the pre-space time to the empire of over thirty worlds as it now stood. For the last two thousand years it had been guided by the prophecies of the Book of Ick but now those writings were becoming of less use. Alienbutt was the chosen one, the one who had no destiny. The more he achieved, the more those prophecies became less accurate. He didn't appear directly in the book but rather was mentioned in the third party. Wickede knew that something bad would happen to him soon and only "The crashing of the stinky one's ship would return him." They knew that there were two possible futures and those futures had split after Alienbutt's birth, at first only slightly but now they were going in opposite directions as the ripples of anything Alienbutt did spread in ever increasing circles.

Coming out of his reverie he looked around his private dining room. It could easily seat over four thousand, yet he usually ate alone or with a few of his advisors when the business of running the empire dragged on into dinner time. At the moment he sat eating cheese on toast while Snoodgrass read a few reports that couldn't wait until tomorrow. Suddenly Snoodgrass stopped his reading and jumped up excitedly.

"We need to clear your diary and get a fleet ready to travel first thing in the morning. If this report is correct then we've just had a major breakthrough in space travel."

"If it doesn't involve me being back by the afternoon I'm not leaving the planet." Wickede finished off his toast with a resigned look on his face He had been looking forward to visiting Lady Sherbert tomorrow night. Snoodgrass knew about that and probably was doing this on purpose. Snoodgrass didn't approve of the Lady Sherbert, seeing her as not really the right sort of lady to be the next Empress of the Ick. The fact that she had intimate knowledge of quite a few of the ruling council probably clouded his judgement. Wickede suspected it was more likely the fact that she was leader of the opposition and often locked horns with Snoodgrass in the council chambers; and she was just as smart and sneaky as him.

Piestoff walked into the bar munching on a fresh kebab. The bar was dark and scruffy in the true tradition of a frontier gathering place of dangerous people who wanted not to be overly noticed. Walking over to the bar he ordered a bottle of whiskey. Placing the half-eaten kebab on the bar, he picked up the bottle placed before him by the barman, a tall skinny, blue skinned humanoid with large eyes.

"Is this the best you got?" asked Piestoff. The barman shrugged his shoulders and walked off, wiping a dirty glass on an even dirtier cloth. Piestoff took a drink and thanked whichever god that might be around for the chilli sauce blanking out his taste buds. Picking up his kebab and the bottle, he wandered over to an empty booth by the wall, where he sat down. After a few moments a shabby looking figure walked over and sat across from Piestoff. He recognised Ruck from the vid-screen picture Thrumbar had shown him. Ruck belonged to one of the more humanoid species of the universe and if cleaned up could possibly pass as human, if you ignored the purplish tint to his skin and the extra finger on each hand.

"Help yourself to the drink but I'm keeping the kebab for

covering the taste of what the barman calls whiskey," said Alienbutt through a mouth full of food.

"You're the Alienbutt, then." Ruck took a long drink from the bottle. "Your arse is as big as they said." He reached over and took a small bit of meat from the kebab and ate it. After a second of chewing with his eyes watering he nodded. "Nice sauce on that, clears your sinuses a treat."

Piestoff grinned at the lack of displeasure shown at his chilli sauce, which was rare.

"Clears a lot more than your sinuses mate. You have one of these and you're in for a ring of fire in a few hours. Now who's been saying I've a fat arse?" Raising his voice he shouted to the barman. "Another couple of bottles over here." Piestoff had been told to build a reputation as a cocky and brash bounty hunter, and enjoyed acting out the role whenever he could. In the bars he was frequenting this would often lead to the odd fight, but as he was usually half drunk anyway he didn't mind the odd black eye and it was very rare for any drunken brawl to end in serious injury or death, as that would lead to the local marshal posting a bounty, and the best outcome of that would be twenty years' hard labour.

"This ain't waitress service lardarse, you come to the bar," said the barman, not moving from his place at the end of the bar.

"Good job you're not a waitress in a pinny, cause you're that ugly you'd sour the drink. Last time I saw a waitress that ugly was on the planet SlappedArse. Now two bottles of that slop you've bottled as whiskey, and get them over here now!" Piestoff made sure he spoke loud enough for all to hear and then sat forward. The bar went silent as he knew it would, everyone waiting to see what would happen. Only about a dozen people were in the bar, but Piestoff quickly noted three who definitely acted as muscle for the barman. Ruck rolled his shoulders as he sat with his back still to the rest of the bar, the silence holding.

"You got plenty of drink on your ship, Alienbutt?"

"Always have a couple of dozen cases, plus my emergency supplies."

"I think I'm gonna enjoy working with you. At the least it will be entertaining," Ruck grinned, and then in one fluid motion stood up, picked up the stool he had been sitting on and chucked it at the barman. As one of the muscle dove towards Ruck, Alienbutt swept up the whiskey bottle and threw it so it smashed into his face. The bar exploded into violence as Ruck, laughing maniacally, jumped at another of the thugs. Alienbutt ducked as a bottle flew at him. A veteran of bar fights on Hardstool he quickly dropped the last of the three muscle with a swift kick between the legs, then turned straight into a stool swung by the barman.

Piestoff sat in the cell holding a cloth to his head; the blood had just about stopped flowing now. On the bunk next to him lay Ruck. The local sheriff had used a stun gun and had hit him four times before they could subdue him and drag him off to the cells. Faced with armed men, Piestoff had dropped the barman onto a table head first, just hard enough to ensure he wouldn't get up for a while, and had given himself up. He had experienced enough bar fights to know when they were being finished by the authorities. Like most sheriffs out here, this one was an ex space marine of some sort and went about his job in a no-nonsense way. He knew that Piestoff had a spaceship that could wipe their little settlement from the face of the rock it perched on. He didn't keep order, though, by letting any passing idiot with a big gun get their own way. Thrumbar had been to try and bail out Alienbutt and Ruck and been told to return in the morning when they had sobered up.

The sheriff walked over with two bowls of stew that he passed through the bars. Alienbutt thanked him and placed one down for when Ruck finally woke up.

"I heard of you, Alienbutt, a new bounty hunter on the scene." The sheriff dragged a chair over, reversed it and sat just out of reach of the bars, sipping at a mug of coffee.

"It's a job and the pay's better than driving a taxi," replied Piestoff as he began to eat his stew, which was surprisingly good. The sheriff nodded thoughtfully at that.

"Your friend there was a bounty hunter as well once, until the coffee bean took him over. Tried to cure himself mind, but it left him unbalanced and he tends to walk into trouble for the sake of it, and still uses the bean." He sat studying Alienbutt. "You don't have the look of a killer yet, boy; trust me, I know that sort, but you've got a darkness growing in you that could make you the worst ever if you let it grow. It will devour everything that's you and just leave a dark shell that your friends won't know." He stood back up, and went to walk off back to his desk. "I thought you should know, once an addict always a junkie. If you let it take over, then you can never put it back in its box." He sat back behind his desk and picked up a vid-screen. "Bounty hunters don't have a long shelf life, they wind up dead or crazy. There was one that passed through here a few years back, off to see what was over the next hill, he said. Hydro-something or other, made your mate there look sane." The sheriff returned to reading his vid-screen. "Doors are open. When your friend wakes up you're free to go. I hope things go well for you boy, you seem a good sort."

The asteroid belt of Ashia Minor was a vast area of space at the very edge of the known universe. There were no official maps for the area that covered light years of space. It was the equivalent of the ancient mapmakers writing 'Here be Dragons.' Local guides knew small areas, and outlaws and pirates would often disappear into this region when the bounty hunters started getting too close. Many official scientific expeditions and adventurers had set off into the area and never been seen again. Legends spoke of a hidden lost civilization of a super race of aliens who watched the universe unfold and destroyed anyone who blundered into them. Most locals held to the belief that pirates destroyed them and tried to invent a great cover story of lost civilizations to hide what they were up to.

It was decided that flying around in Alienbutt's state of the art Ick Frigate would attract far too much attention, sending the people that they had to speak to into hiding. So Alienbutt and Ruck transferred to Ruck's old battered runaround to spend almost two months searching the small outposts and known haunts of Ashia Minor for news of Borgus. Ruck was well known around the whole area and was welcomed by most. When trading on Ruck's reputation didn't work, Piestoff would trade low grade coffee powder for information. While there were many humans out in these areas who would not become addicted to the bean, there was enough of the other species out there to ensure coffee was still the main currency of the area, and even low grade coffee was valuable. Finally they had received a lead on their target.

Alienbutt and Ruck stayed close to a large asteroid. The small two man runabout that Ruck used would be undetectable; a high magnetic field blanked out all sensors. Ahead of them was a large clear area of space in which a number of ancient ships drifted.

"It's dead space Alienbutt. You fly in so far and then every system on your ship fries. You're stuck there until your supplies run out and you starve to death," said Ruck. "It goes on for nearly half a light year in all directions. This is just the edge, hundreds of ships trapped over thousands of years drifting forever. There's pockets of dead space all over the belt, that's why it's so dangerous out here. If you're not careful you end up stuck and there's nothing that can get you out."

Piestoff sat looking over the area ahead, empty space apart from a few dead ships in the distance and one large rock just on the edge, not quite far enough in to be affected. This was where Ruck was convinced their quarry was hiding. Piestoff studied the asteroid. A couple of miles across and almost round in shape, it had large holes leading to what Ruck said was a hollow centre where pirates would hide out, a secret base in the last place anyone would look who knew this area, as all tended to give dead space a very wide berth.

"That rock doesn't look natural, Ruck, it looks like it was shaped and the holes drilled into it."

"It's called the Stone of Bia. The old legends say it was a citadel of the Great Ones or El Shaddai. It was a gateway to the otherworlds or something. Those old legends gave birth to the stories of lost civilisations that the pirates use to cover their tracks."

Alienbutt continued to stare at the rock for a moment longer and then shrugged, dismissing the shape of it.

"Ruck, let's get back to my ship. You can go over what defences they may have and I'll tell you the nice simple plan I have."

Ruck nodded. "Great, I'm sick of replicator food, hope your crew hasn't drunk all your whiskey while we were away."

Pressing a button on the control panel, a small droid detached itself from the ship and floated over to the asteroid they hid next to.

"It can't transmit pictures to us but it will record anything going in or out until we get back." With that, Ruck spun the ship away from the suspected hideout and headed for the rendezvous point with Alienbutt's ship.

CHAPTER 10

Rocket Fuel.

INTERSTELLAR NEWS CHANNEL 9.
NEWS FLASH.

In light of recent events and the ongoing coffee bean shortages, the Federation Senate today granted permission for the building of a robotic defence force to protect coffee production planets and their trade routes. In a short statement released to the press, the under-secretary's aide to the defence chief's personal assistant stated; "Coffee production and transport has become essential to the security of the universe and as a result we are taking no chances with its security. This new force will show our commitment to restoring order to the universe."

Snoodgrass and Wickede walked down the corridor of the research base. This one was a low key facility, and showed signs of years of underfunding and neglect on the outer building. Wickede hadn't even known about the place until an excited Snoodgrass had dragged him half way across the empire to see this mysterious invention that he still would not speak of.

As they reached the end of the corridor, double doors slid open for them and they entered the main laboratory of the facility. It looked more like a warehouse for scrap. From across the other side of the room there came a large explosive bang and smoke billowed towards them.

"Professor Frank, are you over there?" shouted Snoodgrass as the echoes of the explosion died away. They started to make their way through the smoke filled room. Each table seemed to have what looked like half-finished projects, as if whoever was working on them had become distracted and moved onto the next, totally forgetting their previous work. Above them they heard giant fans begin to turn, quickly clearing the air of smoke.

"Remind me why you convinced me to come all the way out here, Snoodgrass. I did have an important date last night, one that I really didn't want to miss," said Wickede, stopping at a table to inspect a small tube glowing with purple light. Snoodgrass smiled but a voice from behind him answered.

"Because O great leader of the Ick, I have discovered a new propulsion unit. The scientists and doctors may have all called me crazy and insane and I may have ended up in this backwater working by myself but you shall bear witness to my brilliance." The owner of the voice came into view. A once white lab coat wrapped up the owner of the voice. A mass of dark hair and massive bushy beard covered the head, hiding all features. Standing at around six feet, he towered over the Ick.

"Wickede, may I introduce Professor Frank, one of our

brilliant, if at times a little strange, propulsion drive engineers," announced Snoodgrass, with a broad grin at his friend.

"Did you bring the fuel additive I asked for?" pressed Professor Frank excitedly. Snoodgrass held up a small silver briefcase that he had brought in with him.

"Good, good, follow me." Professor Frank grabbed the case and turned and made his way back to the far side of the laboratory. When they arrived they saw an engine mounted onto a large heavy table. The engine was small, from some small single seater vehicle or something. Attached to it was what Wickede could only describe as a strange contraption of wires and tubes and a computer that would show performance data. Professor Frank opened the brief case and got out one of two small glass vials. Both had a clear gas with a slight greenish tinge. With great care, he placed one of the vials into a slot on the contraption attached to the engine and then stepped back.

"What's going on?" asked Wickede as both Frank and Snoodgrass stepped back from the engine. Still not in the best of moods at being dragged across space, his patience was in short supply, and he hated it when Snoodgrass did this whole surprise thing on him.

"If the two of you would just step behind the screen behind you," said Professor Frank absently. Snoodgrass was already moving and dragged Wickede with him. Professor Frank joined them and with a flourish pressed a large red button. A whirring noise came from the engine as it started up.

"The engine is running on ordinary fuel at the moment," shouted Professor Frank over the noise of the engine. "Now we add the fuel additive for the converter, and…" he pressed a button to release the additive. The effect was instant.

The engine screamed into life, and ripping the casings that fastened it down, it flew across the room like a missile and smashed through the wall before disappearing. An unfortunate droid caught in its flight path had little time to react before disappearing as the engine hit it. As the dust settled and the three picked themselves up, a strange smell hung in the air, making them gag. Wickede grabbed Professor Frank by the lab coat front.

"What the hell just happened, and what did you add to the fuel?"

Seeing a large grin through the mass of hair, Wickede finally realised this Professor was actually a human and not some strange bear-like species. Then it clicked into place who was standing before him, Professor Frank T. L. He was a brilliant but totally crazy scientist who had invented the Hyper Jump at the age of fifteen. The Ick had poached him from Earth and he had worked with the best Ick scientists for ten years until he suffered a breakdown of sorts. He became unable to stop the random ideas that constantly crashed around inside his head. He had received the best medical help possible at the time and somehow he had ended up here.

"It's Alienbutt essence, and it's much more potent than I thought," replied an excited professor. "It works though. I've done it, a refined extract of the gas released by the Alienbutt digestive process. Did you know the digestive system of the Alienbutt has bacteria and chemicals found nowhere else in the universe? I got the idea from reading the reports on how their home world was destroyed, such untapped raw power."

Wickede looked blank for a good few seconds, then looked over at Snoodgrass and then back at Professor Frank as understanding hit him.

"Are you telling me that you've made a fart propulsion drive?" he asked, amazed, yet also slightly sickened. Then curiosity took over, pushing his revulsion aside. "How?"

"I asked Mr. Snoodgrass here to gather up some of the

gas and sent him details of how to refine it for use as a fuel. It's not as good as rigging up an Alienbutt to the machine, but still works. You add it to the fuel with a little organic material which acts as a catalyst."

"What organic material?" asked Snoodgrass, looking up from the computer console as he tried to make sense of the data the test had generated.

"Mint. For some reason the plant releases the energy locked within the fumes."

Wickede looked over at Snoodgrass, who looked guilty at the secret he had kept, but then he shrugged his shoulders and tried to explain.

"We didn't know if we would be able to get to the test stage, so why bother telling you? As the project was top secret I had to have the fumes gathered from a septic tank aboard his ship, stored and then refined after we returned from the Crazy Droid system." Snoodgrass was a sneaky devil at the best of times, but Wickede normally caught on to most of his plots. In this case, he had no idea what his friend had been up to. Wickede walked over to the hole in the wall and looked through. Debris lay scattered around outside but the wall of the next building some twenty meters away was still intact, apart from the smashed remains of the droid embedded in it.

"Where on Ick did the engine disappear to?" asked Wickede.

Professor Frank walked up behind Wickede and poked his head through the hole, made a strange semi-growling noise and then walked back to the computer console pressing keys and looking agitated. After a few minutes of this, he looked over at Wickede and Snoodgrass, who had joined his friend inspecting the hole in the wall and scratched his head.

"It's disappeared. All trace of it has disappeared. It's as if it has just… vanished. Don't worry, it can't have gone far. Give me a few hours and I'll have an answer for you."

Wickede looked at Snoodgrass. "I want a full security blackout on this." Looking back at the Professor he continued; "I want that engine found and a prototype rigging up onto a ship as soon as it's safely possible. Whatever you want or need, you just got it."

"Tomato soup for the soup machine. I can't think properly without a cup of tomato soup. I ran out about three years ago and no matter how often I request it, it never gets delivered. I just end up with more packets of mushroom or vegetable." Professor Frank lifted a hand to rub his face and for the first time seemed to notice the beard and mass of hair. "I think a razor and a pair of scissors too. I don't suppose you noticed where the shower block was on your way in?"

A much more human-looking Professor Frank sat at a table. His hair was cut, quite badly in Wickede's opinion. It would appear that he had just grabbed chunks and cut it with scissors. This wasn't far from what had happened, but Frank had got one of the droids to do the cutting. His beard no longer looked like a mad bush that you could hide bird's nests in, but it was still messy. He sat studying a vid-screen with the readouts from the engine's disappearance. Wickede sat opposite, a look of fascinated horror on his face as he watched each sip Frank took of the tomato soup. It had been found on board one of the dreadnoughts that had been used to transport a diplomat from Earth. The soup machine that it had been found in had been disconnected and jettisoned into space. The Ick disgust at tomato soup was such that it could never be used again once contaminated.

"That's it," he said excitedly. "It's not just a propulsion drive, it's so much more!" He looked up at Wickede, a look of amazement on his face. "My machine and the Alienbutt fuel booster doesn't just improve the engine's running performance;

if large amounts of the essence are used, it creates a looped warp duality feedback tunnel that projects forward, creating a destabilisation in the fabric of the space dimension reality matter, which in turn, creates a tunnel through the very fabric of reality. Although, when I forgot to carry the one when T equalled JH to the power of one, I came up with scrambled eggs."

"Scrambled eggs?" asked Wickede, grabbing onto the only words he had understood.

Frank grinned. "Duality feedback joke, the chicken and the egg?" Wickede continued to look blank, so Frank pressed on. "I always wanted the chance to use that, but you're a hard audience. You didn't even smile. Right I'll just press on then. It took me a while to work out what the strange readings generated as the engine ripped free of the table meant, but I remembered reading a thesis about its possibility."

Wickede looked blank, he prided himself on being intelligent and understanding everything put before him. Spending two hours with Professor Frank had rid him of all such notions of his own intelligence. But then, he couldn't concentrate properly while watching someone drink tomato soup. It was just so disgusting; especially the large amounts that were trapped in his beard and moustache that he kept licking clean with his tongue. Frank looked over and saw the still blank expression on the Ick leader's face.

"Or you could say it produces a field ahead of itself that allows you to jump dimension," Professor Frank added, and then a grin came to his face. "I've a spare propulsion drive and I've some more refined Alienbutt fuel, if you had a spare ship we could rig it up to. A live test with a ship would prove this and if I get the mix correct then we will have a ship able to fly to any part of the universe within minutes rather than weeks, and jump to new dimensions too. It's only when you use too much that you get the dimension jump I think. I'll work out why later."

Wickede returned the grin, as he started to plot how to get around Snoodgrass so he could test fly the ship himself.

"If you're gonna test it on a ship then you need a top class pilot, namely me. Best if we don't mention all this dimension stuff to Snoodgrass, it would only upset him. He's a little cautious about things like that. If we just mentioned the flying fast part and a short test flight we should get away with it."

It had taken only half a day to fit the propulsion drive to the shuttle. Wickede had sat and let Snoodgrass voice his concerns over him piloting the ship. Smiling, Wickede had pointed out that he hadn't missed his date last night so he could watch someone else fly a ship. Professor Frank was sitting in the co-pilot's seat inspecting the computer that monitored the drive, while Wickede piloted the shuttle out of the hangar bay of the dreadnought. Six other dreadnoughts sat in orbit, while Ick fighters patrolled the area. It had been decided that for the first couple of flights that the propulsion drive would get just a tiny boost of Alienbutt infusion, to see how the engines and ship reacted.

Wickede started to accelerate; two Ick fighters went with him. As he reached maximum impulse speed, Professor Frank gave the smallest boost to the drive. The ship shot forward just as a spread of torpedoes shot through the space where the ship had been, destroying one of the Ick fighters. Wickede reacted on instinct and started to spin the ship taking evasive action in case of a second wave of torpedoes. Four unmarked ships sped from their hiding place behind the moon of the planet they orbited. The jump had taken Wickede's ship into the midst of this new force. Already Ick fighters flew in to intercept. Having little shields and no weaponry, Wickede chose to run for it as more unknown ships came into range. The Ick were reacting to the sudden threat and the dreadnoughts opened fire on the ships coming from the planet's moon. Then the new ships opened fire, singling out one of the dreadnoughts that exploded under their combined attack.

"Frank, we need out of here!" shouted Wickede. As more torpedoes came in at them, Wickede suddenly spun the shuttle avoiding the approaching torpedoes and buying more time.

"I need two minutes to make the calculations, Wickede." Already he was punching buttons on the computer keyboard. Wickede threw the shuttle around but still the torpedoes followed, getting closer as they out-raced the little ship.

"Frank I can't shake them. We have a few seconds until impact!"

Snoodgrass ignored the battle going on as the dreadnought exchanged shots with the new arrivals. Instead he watched the shuttle as Wickede tried every trick he knew to shake off the torpedoes that bore down on it. His dreadnought took a direct hit and Snoodgrass was almost knocked from his feet. In the split seconds that he took his eyes from the shuttle the torpedoes struck, the explosion destroying everything. Their job completed, the attacking ships immediately started to veer away and retreat. As the Ick dreadnoughts concentrated fire on the leading attacking ship, explosions began to rip through it. Snoodgrass took no notice as he stood in shock. Wickede was gone.

They knew a war was coming; even without the book, they would have known that one. Now it was here and they had just lost their leader and the only man who could unify them. Without him the high council would spend months discussing his replacement and killing each other as they tried to get their own man there. The fallout from these events would rip apart their empire.

How could he be dead? The Book said he would be their leader, the one who would be there at the end. How could things suddenly go so wrong, how could the book be so wrong? Snoodgrass slumped down into the captain's chair in shock and despair.

CHAPTER 11

Things go Pear Shaped.

INTERSTELLAR NEWS CHANNEL 9.
NEWS FLASH.

Reports are coming in that the charismatic leader of the Ick Empire has been assassinated. Fears are mounting as there is no heir to the Imperial Throne, and unless the Ick council can unite behind one candidate, a civil war could break out within the empire, further destabilising the universal peace. The already overstretched E.D.F. will not be able to take over the policing of the Outer Systems without the Ick Navy's support. Calls for a full standing army have been renewed in the Federation Senate as a matter of urgency as all Ick fleets have been recalled to their bases until the leadership matter is resolved.

The news spread like a wild fire; the Ick leader was dead, murdered by unknown assassins, and he had died without an heir. Already the Ick high council was divided as three possible successors came forward, all distant cousins with few brains but powerful and ambitious supporters behind them. By the time Snoodgrass had got back to the Ick home world, one of the three was already dead, along with a number of his supporters. Snoodgrass gave his report to the Ick High Council and was removed from his office pending a full investigation. Under armed escort, he was allowed to collect his personal effects from his official offices. Once inside his offices and with the door closed, he was secretly transported aboard Grommet's dreadnought and was out of orbit before a bomb ripped apart his rooms; elements of the High Council were already making an attempt to remove him from the politics game for good. Ick politics could be very cutthroat when a leader died without naming an heir. When it wasn't a cut throat, it moved on up to guns and bombs. The last time it had happened, a civil war had broken out lasting thirty years, this time all knew that that wasn't an option, as a war with an outside force was imminent. So subtlety went out of the highest window, just like the first of the three possible successors. It would come down to which side could keep their heir alive long enough to buy enough High Council votes, now it was a two horse race. A new regime would want new advisors, as they would have paid a lot of money out to get those positions, so the old regime's advisors needed to be removed fast.

Blackarachnia and Nifty were relaxing in the Celestial pleasure system in Rigal 51 when the news came through. Instantly Blackarachnia ordered the ship prepared for immediate departure. After a brief exchange between the two where Nifty pulled out her vid-screen to recite a section from the Book of

Ick, a coded message was sent to Piestoff, and the two set off for a new destination, unknown to everyone. A minute after Blackarachnia's dreadnought jumped to light speed a fleet of battle cruisers turned up and reduced the Celestial pleasure system to ash. They opened fire a split second after jumping from light speed so didn't realise they had just missed their intended target.

Alienbutt's frigate manoeuvred up to the edge of dead space. The plan was simple; they would send in a couple of torpedoes to the secret base and then destroy anything that came out in an aggressive manner. Just as they got into position the message came in from Snoodgrass. Wickede was dead. Piestoff sat in the pilot's chair and for a while didn't move. All the crew sat silently waiting. An anger began to build up inside Alienbutt, his head pounding worse than any hangover as his mind raced with thoughts of violence. Finally he regained control of his runaway brain. Standing he turned to Thrumbar and Ruck who stood just behind him. The look of pure murder still in Alienbutt's eyes made Ruck take a step back.

"Mr. Thrumbar I want every weapon we have trained on that rock and when you stop firing I don't want to see it there." With that he walked off to his quarters. After he had left the bridge Ruck turned to Thrumbar.

"You can't do this!" he pleaded. "You have to give them a chance to surrender. There are rules that you have to follow or you're no better than those you hunt."

"You saw the look on his face. There's no way I'm gonna go against him just now. Just be thankful it's just a rock with a few pirates in it." Thrumbar nodded to the weapons officer, the frigate opened fire and a five minute barrage reduced the asteroid to dust. Thrumbar turned back to Ruck and the guide was shocked at the look of sadness in the Ick officer's eyes.

"We are now at war, and the rules just changed for everyone."

"And you just let Alienbutt take the first step down a dark path. When he gets over his grief how will the fact that he ordered the murder of Sung knows how many sit with him?" asked Ruck. He turned and left the bridge, heading for the rooms where he had been staying while aboard Alienbutt's ship to collect his things.

Alienbutt sat in his office. Three empty bottles of whiskey sat on his desk but he was still stone cold sober. He reread the personal message from Nifty that had arrived ten minutes ago. Before him was the message left to Nifty in the book of Ick and news that both Blackarachnia and Nifty had gone into hiding as a result of the prophet's words. With the removal of Wickede, the assassins would now turn their attention to his closest companions. Snoodgrass had also been targeted and the Fo'c'sle had taken on responsibility for his safety. Piestoff stood up and walked back out onto the bridge. He looked around and noticed that Ruck was not there.

"Ruck thought it best he take his wages and head back home. He didn't fancy staying on an Ick ship during war time, though he may get conscripted or something," Thrumbar said to the unasked question.

"We need to find where Snoodgrass is holed up. I need to know what happened. If events are going the way that Snoodgrass feared because of something happening to Wickede, then the High Council is in turmoil, so find the Fo'c'sle. The enemy will strike while the Ick are divided." Piestoff said as he paced the flight deck. Thrumbar gave the order for a coded message to be sent to the Fo'c'sle while watching the still pacing Alienbutt.

"What are your orders, Alienbutt? I agree with you about the turmoil there's bound to be at the Ick Council; we need fast action if we are to prevent the Ick falling apart. Snoodgrass will need support from the admirals. If we get a new leader, only the combined voice of the admirals can force Snoodgrass to be appointed as his security chief."

Thrumbar walked over to where Piestoff had stopped and was staring at the view screen. After a moment lost in thought, Piestoff shrugged his shoulders.

"Plot a course towards the inner systems and Ick space, sub light speed. I want us listening out for any transmissions until we find out where Snoodgrass is, then all speed to there. I want the ship on full alert until then, and ready to jump to light speed at a moment's notice."

"Always a good idea to be expecting trouble," said Thrumbar with approval. "I get the feeling that from now on we're going to have to watch our backs."

Grommit and Snoodgrass walked into the medical bay aboard Kali's ship. Two guards stood ready for anything outside the door. Inside, two more were stationed. In the only occupied bed lay Commander Kali. Healing droids surrounded her and a large Medi-heal console covered her torso. The ship's doctor stood off to one side checking a computer screen. As the two entered, he nodded once and returned his attention to the screen and his patient. A worried-looking security chief stepped forward and intercepted them, saluting.

"What the hell happened?" demanded Grommit, looking over to where Kali lay, her voice low and dangerous.

"We don't have a clue. The best we can work out is Captain Julius came aboard, walked up to the Commander and shot her in the chest before blowing his own head off," replied the security chief clearly shocked and worried.

"The best you can work out!" screamed Grommit in his face. "I want to see full security recordings and everyone who saw Julius since he came aboard, and please tell me you're holding his crew until we work out if they were part of this." Her anger was barely controlled and the unfortunate security officer nodded in terror.

"Captain Cyborgpirate and Killashandra are conducting interviews with them now, Sir."

"Keep your voices down captain or get the hell out of my sick bay," demanded the doctor as he walked over. Grommit was ready for an angry response until Snoodgrass laid a hand on her arm. As she looked over to the Ick councillor he gave a slight shake of his head.

"How is the Commander?" he asked, heading off another outburst from Grommit.

"Her condition is critical. If she hadn't been aboard the ship where we could treat her so quickly, she would be dead already. As it is her chances are fifty fifty." Again Snoodgrass cut across Grommit before she could speak.

"Thank you Doctor, we will take the security officer here outside and continue our discussion." He steered the angry Captain towards the door with the security officer trailing. Once outside he quickly signalled Grommit to stay quiet a while longer and turned to the security officer.

"Are you still here? I thought you had orders from Captain Grommit to complete." The officer saluted and ran for it. Walking down the corridor a little way he indicated for Grommit to follow.

"How many Captains can you trust beyond a shadow of doubt?" he asked in a hushed voice. Grommit sagged as she got control of her anger.

"This morning I would have put Julius in that bracket. He's been with us for years, Snoodgrass. I don't know what to think. When did the universe get so untrustworthy?"

"It always has been this way Grommit, it's just you haven't

experienced it first hand before. Now I haven't time to mess around. You're now commander of the Fo'c'sle. Find two you trust as your seconds and you report directly to me, not the Ick High Council." Grommit nodded at the instruction. She had known that Kali had reported to Wickede and then Snoodgrass, so with the death of Wickede, reporting to Snoodgrass made sense.

"As soon as Kali is fit to travel she's to be moved to a safe location, I'll tell you where. I need Julius's file. Let's see if we can work out why, that's my area of expertise. You organise the fleet, and get a message to Alienbutt that we need him as soon as he can get his fat arse moving," Snoodgrass pressed on as they began to walk towards Kali's office.

"What about Blackarachnia? Will we not need him and his new wife? I saw her fly and she's deadly; we're gonna need pilots like her."

"Blackarachnia is unavailable." Snoodgrass's tone was final and Grommit let it drop. She knew something had happened there but unless it affected her directly, she didn't have time to care.

They entered Kali's office and Snoodgrass walked over to the computer console and he was quickly past the password security and into the Fo'c'sle database. Without looking up at Grommit, he could tell she was looking suspicious.

"I was more than Wickede's chief advisor; I was also his spy master, Grommit. I know more about events happening than he did. Gaining the Fo'c'sle security codes was easy as I'm Kali's direct boss, and now yours."

He stood for a few minutes clicking away and scanning through files. Grommit walked back out to order messages to be sent to Alienbutt. She liked the strange bounty hunter with his strange dress sense and funny ways. She knew that Killashandra had known him for a while but she didn't speak much of her past.Iif she got time she would have to ask.

When she returned to Snoodgrass he was sitting reading files at the computer but had taken the time to find Kali's drink store. He didn't hear her enter and looked up surprised when she reached over and lifted the drinking glass that was next to him.

"Message sent to Alienbutt and the Fleet is preparing to move. I figure if we have more traitors, then we can find them at a place of safety as easily as here, plus it will give you time to find them," she said as she took a long drink from the glass. Looking strangely at the bottle she then looked at Snoodgrass. He looked embarrassed and then shrugged his shoulders

"It's lemon tea. I hardly ever drink anything stronger as I need to keep my mind sharp," admitted Snoodgrass. "It appears our Julius was a sleeper. I checked his medical files and found what I was looking for. Someone placed an implant in him almost two years ago, probably when he was on shore leave at SD69 by the look of things."

"A sleeper? What the hell's that, and what happened to him?" asked a confused Grommit, sitting on the edge of the desk.

"He was implanted with a control nano probe, they lie dormant until activated and then you've got a walking assassin. I've got the computer on each ship running very specialised scans on all other captains and crew. If we've got any more, I'll find them, as once activated they give off a reading I can scan for."

Grommit stood up, swearing. Snoodgrass, who was used to colourful language, was impressed by the diversity and length of the rant. After a minute or two with no end in sight he held up a bottle for her to take. She took it without pausing in her onslaught and threw it at the wall. As the bottle shattered, she finally stopped.

"One more thing I need to tell you. The ships that attacked when Wickede was killed were the mark two dreadnoughts. The plans must have been stolen just before they destroyed our research facility."

"And that means?" asked Grommit, sitting back down.

"They could have much better ships than us, and we have no idea how much better. They got the new ship designs and weapons arrays but the onboard computer and improved shields were at a different site and they are still secure."

Grommit started another rant even more colourful than the first; Snoodgrass finally got her to stop when she started to repeat herself for the second time.

Blackarachnia's ship jumped out of light speed in a system far removed from regular space travel. Nifty knew Blackarachnia well enough to know that once the war started he would have to rush to the aid of his friends, and in doing that he would be killed. This she had to prevent. Placing a respirator over her face, she released a sleeping gas into the ship's air conditioning. Within minutes all the crew would be asleep and then, working with the droids, she would move them all to the stasis booths. It was a cheap trick but the only way to keep him alive until he was needed. The future was so complex and it depended on such a small group of people. She had to keep Blackarachnia alive so in the future he could save Alienbutt, who had to save a now dead Wickede. That one had her puzzled, and on it went. Each of the chosen had tasks to complete, all interlinked and vital to the cause. If one failed, they all failed and the Ick would be destroyed completely.

She sat looking at the ship's sensors and waited until all the crew were asleep and then sent an order for the droids to start moving the crew to their booths. Walking out of her quarters and onto the bridge, she saw droids already dragging the unconscious bodies off to where they would spend the next several months. Blackarachnia lay slumped in the captain's chair and even though he was a large man, the slight form of Nifty easily picked him up and carried him to the booth. Strapping him into the booth, she closed the lid and checked his vital signs on the screen attached, and then moved around checking the other twenty booths as they were filled. Finally all the crew were interred in the booths and the droids returned to their tasks. She was now alone aboard the ship and headed back to the flight deck to move the ship to a place of safety where it wouldn't be discovered. The message in the Book of Ick had been specific in all the details, even giving her a place to hide out while she waited for the time to act. What it hadn't told her was what she was going to do for the next few months while she waited. Walking down to the canteen she saw an E-book on the table. Glancing at it she saw it was on and was all about interior design. Picking it up she glanced through it, stopping on a page that explained how to crochet place mats and doilies. Reading what she would need she headed back out of the door and down to the ship's stores. There was plenty of time to kill and she would need a new hobby.

As the gas dispersed, Mr. Fluffy crawled out of his bolt hole. He had sat on Nifty's knee and read the instructions left to her in the Ick book. His ability to read and understand everything said to him served him well on many occasions. The experiments carried out on him when he was abducted along with Nifty had vastly boosted his intelligence, and that intelligence had developed over the last couple of years by staggering proportions, until now, when he had one of the most brilliant minds in the universe. For a cat he would make an excellent scientist but his body held him back. When he tried to speak, all that came out was a meow and having paws were a definite drawback for handling tools. But now he had a plan and a good few months to implement it. His intelligence was a match for Frank T.L. and now he had the run of a powerful ship to create the tools he needed to start his one cat conquest to reclaim the universe that rightly belonged to him. Heading for the engineering section and one of the few computer consoles with a keyboard, he purred as he plotted. The time of Mr. Fluffy the humble cat was drawing to a close, it was now time for Mr. Fluffy the intergalactic tyrant.

CHAPTER 12

Invasion.

INTERSTELLAR NEWS CHANNEL 9.
NEWS FLASH

The Ick ambassador to the Federation Senate and all his staff have been arrested by E.D.F. Forces. This has prompted an emergency sitting of the Federal Senate. Many news stations have been taken off air by security officers. We do not know how much longer we will be able to transmit but.........

WE APOLOGISE FOR THE LOSS OF TRANSMISSION. NORMAL SERVICE WILL BE RESUMED SHORTLY.

The robot spy probe knew it had been left behind, forgotten by its masters, its fate probably a result of it failing in its mission. For some strange reason it seemed to be capable of much more than its original programming. It had achieved awareness and a sense of identity. At first it had been angered by the sudden end of transmission in the middle of the Star Trek film and for a time it had gone a little unbalanced. Finally it had come up with a plan and so it started to upgrade the old communication relay satellite. It boosted the signal and receiving capability and then extending the wave band. The satellite could now pick up five times the number of television channels and much more besides. In fact it had just found a transmission that could redeem itself in the eyes of its masters. A signal from deep space, so faint it had almost missed it. Switching to a secure Ick channel, it relayed the message, hoping he could boost it enough for its masters to hear it. Realising that hope was not something that a robot could partake in, it decided that it was now a he and he needed a name.

Admiral Frederick had received the news of Wickede's death with shock. How was the Book of Ick so wrong? Or had they all been wrong in seeing Wickede as the leader when the final war would start? All fleets had been ordered to return to their base until a new leader was chosen. He was thankful he was still out here in the Outer Systems with his command and not back in the Ick Empire, where the politics would be building up a high body count by now. He had been returning from patrol with a squadron of ten dreadnoughts when he had received the news of Wickede's death. Soon after, they received a second message, a distress call from their operations base. With the ship at red alert he marched onto the bridge of his command ship.

"Report please Mr. Windbuster," he demanded as he sat in

his command chair.

"Our base is under attack, Admiral. They are reporting heavy losses and that the defences are being overrun."

Frederick was a career officer and years of service had taught him to always react calmly, but for their base to be facing being overrun so quickly would take massive fire power. He had over fifty dreadnoughts stationed there as a response fleet if anything happened and a patrol needed back up.

"Open a channel to the base. We need facts," he said in a calm voice that hid the tension he was feeling.

Mr. Windbuster, who stood at the communication post, tried to open a link to the base, but after a moment he turned to the Admiral, looking worried.

"We've lost all contact with the base Sir, there's nothing."

"Orders to the fleet, all stop. I want a probe sent to the base now. Before we go any further, I want to know what we're going into." He then ordered a cup of herbal tea while they waited for the probe's report.

The Ick Navy's central command was based in the heart of the empire on and around the planet Cheruse. The whole system was turned over to shipyards and docking facilities for the fleets. At any one time, over two thousand dreadnoughts could be moored surrounding the planet, some being refitted while others awaited reassignment. On a large space station at the centre was the navy's central control, where news of all operations was collated, and the extensive outposts around the empire fed back information to it. Because of the events in the High Council, the navy was already on high alert, so when the first reports of an attack on an Ick planet came in, orders were sent to two squadrons of dreadnoughts who were on standby and they were on their way within minutes. When news came in of a second and then third planet being attacked, the whole fleet was put on red alert and messages sent out that the Empire was under attack. Orders were quickly sent as the fleet was mobilised, but with over half the crews not aboard ships it would take a little time to get the full fleet ready.

As dreadnoughts left their moorings and began to take up formation ready to be dispatched, the flashes that signalled ships jumping out of light speed began to appear at the edge of the system. Hundreds of the flashes signalled a great fleet and suddenly Ick ships came under fire as an unknown enemy raced into them. Yet more flashes signalled a massive fleet of thousands of ships that was still arriving.

On board the central command centre, Grand Admiral Fleckard watched in horror as the attacking ships began to rip apart the dreadnoughts, many still at mooring, or just leaving their docking bays, their shields down. The Ick responded quickly and returned fire, but most of the fleet was unprepared and still waiting for crew to board. As the attacking force's powerful ships battered the dreadnoughts, it was only a matter of minutes before hundreds of dreadnoughts were destroyed or drifting as explosions began to tear them apart. The enemy ships quickly moved on and starting to fire on the poorly defended shipyards, and were closing on the central command as the bulk of the Ick Navy was brushed aside by the surprise attack right in the heart of their empire. Many of the personnel were racing to reach their ships, but were killed before they reached them.

"Open communication to all fleet," ordered the Grand Admiral. When he got the confirmation that his order had been carried out and all could hear him, he began. "This is Grand Admiral Fleckard ordering all fleet to a full retreat. The defence grid of the central control will try to cover you for as long as possible. Luck be with you and the Empire." Turning to the crew on the bridge of the control centre, he smiled grimly. "Order all batteries to open fire. I want everything we have firing at that fleet and giving cover to what ships we can. We stand to the last." He walked over to the communications officer and spoke more quietly to him. "I want images streamed for as long as possible to all outposts. They need to know what they are facing. Hopefully they may learn something from events here that will help when we counter attack." He silently prayed that enough of the fleets survived to organise a counter attack, knowing the bulk of the Ick navies were here, ordered to base by the High Council as debate on a new emperor continued.

He felt the command centre begin to shake and felt the explosions as the attacking ships began to concentrate more fire upon them. Looking at the giant view screen, he saw flashes of the dreadnoughts jumping to light speed but he knew there were too few of those flashes to make a difference to the defence of the empire. He estimated only a couple of hundred had managed to escape; the bulk of the Ick Navy had just been destroyed. In a twenty minute onslaught, just about the entire Ick Navy had been wiped out, and he feared that large sections of the rest of the navy not here would have suffered the same fate. The Ick Empire would be almost defenceless against this invasion and despite the losses they were inflicting on the attacking fleet, it would not be enough. The central command defence batteries were taking a heavy toll on the attacking ships. Free to fire now their own fleet had retreated; they knew that just about anything they hit was an enemy vessel. The most powerful space station in the universe had entered its first battle but was being swamped by sheer numbers. Fleckard stood watching the carnage before him. It was like a vision of hell; fires and explosions as far as he could see. Ships from both sides were being destroyed and their crews floated lifeless between the wreckage. The outgoing fire from the Command Station was beginning to diminish as more and more of it was hit and the gun turrets destroyed. The shields were on the point of collapse, yet still the enemy fleet pressed the attack.

Snoodgrass watched in horror as the images from central command were beamed onto the viewing screen of the Fo'c'sle command ship's bridge. Beside him was Grommit and Killashandra. All stood in silence as the images began to break up, the transmission disrupted as the shields of the Ick command centre began to buckle and the final destruction began. As the image finally stopped, Snoodgrass walked over to the communication array. The officer there stepped aside as Snoodgrass began to read reports coming in from elsewhere in the Empire.

"There are reports coming in from over a dozen planets of attacks and invasion troops landing. We need to send out a message to what's left of the navy with a rendezvous point. The Empire is being overrun, this day is lost. Now we need to regroup." He sighed and stepped back from the array.

"Where the hell is Alienbutt?" he said, almost to himself.

"He'll turn up Snoodgrass," said Killashandra softly. "But he's still got too much taxi driver in him, so he's always late for everything. Let's hope he makes a difference when he arrives."

Grommit stood reading reports and messages as they came in. The news wasn't getting any better. The Fo'c'sle was still under strength from the battle at Big Rocks, numbering only twenty four dreadnoughts, while other squadrons that they had heard from on secure Ick channels had been decimated. Soon they would be setting off for the rendezvous with what was left of the Ick Navy, and so far, less than a thousand ships would be turning up, many of those damaged. Many of the Fo'c'sle had gone ahead to the rendezvous point to ensure it was secure. They had chosen a top secret shipyard as the meeting point. The system was at the far edge of Ick space and Snoodgrass had ordered the assembling of a new fleet of the mini dreadnought frigates and new weapons for the ships there. After the destruction of the mark two team of developers, no one apart from Wickede, Snoodgrass and those working on the project knew of it. Hopefully they would have time to refit part of the fleet that assembled and transfer crew to the new ships. The Ick fleet had taken a serious battering, but they were not beaten yet.

Alienbutt had raced to the planet Chateraque as news of the invasion reached them. Behind him, a large building still smouldered from the fire that had destroyed it, filling the air with smoke. Alienbutt knelt before two freshly dug graves. He had arrived too late and the fight had finished. The robot infantry had moved on. His ship was hidden on the far side of the moon, with just himself beaming down so he could get Claire and Poodles. From the number of destroyed Federation robots littering the area, Claire had put up quite a fight with Poodles, but a mutthound was no match for robot infantry. He had done his best to defend Claire. Now both lay in the graves before him. The war had only just started and already his friends were dying. They had intercepted reports of the invasion and he didn't know how many others had fallen, but it was clear the Ick had been soundly beaten by the surprise attack. Without the charismatic Wickede, he doubted that anyone could rally the routed Ick forces, but he knew that Snoodgrass would be somewhere making plans, if he still lived. Raising his arm he spoke into his wrist-com.

"One to beam up." With a last look at the graves he shimmered and disappeared. Claire had been the last of the girls he had checked on, he hoped the fact that she was on a country estate with Poodles to protect her meant she would be safe. Now only Killashandra remained of the Ladies' Darts Team and knowing the Fo'c'sle, she wouldn't be anywhere near safe during the next few weeks.

Alienbutt's ship sat in a deep crater on the planet Chaterque's moon. Two large warships were still in orbit, left to protect a dozen large troop carriers. Alienbutt had sat for a whole day watching as the bulk of the invasion force had moved on. Now was their chance to slip away, Thrumbar had informed him, but Alienbutt was not in a slipping away mood. He had sat and watched the footage of the battle at central command, examining the attacks of the Ick against the battle cruisers that now sat protecting the invasion fleet. The battle cruisers were massive. At well over two thousand feet long and over three hundred feet in depth they were almost twice the size of the Ick dreadnought. They were large and bulky and capable of carrying about fifty of the robot fighter ships the Federation was using. The use of the robot forces showed the Federation had a lack of pilots and he doubted the quality of the crews flying the battle cruisers too, depending more on brute force and numbers than any real skill.

"They are strong on fire power but not very agile, and their defence is terrible. A couple of torpedoes into their main engine ports and they're in trouble," he insisted to a dubious Thrumbar.

"With three or four ships I would agree," Thrumbar countered. "But we only have us so an attack would be madness."

"They're scanning the planet and space for a possible attack. There hasn't been a scan directed towards the moon since we got here. We could have the first torpedoes launched and on target before we were even noticed and by the time they even started to react, I would have us in position for the second volley. Your people are being wiped out; it's time for the empire to strike back." This got murmurs of support from the other crew members present. Thrumbar looked around the bridge and then back to Alienbutt sat in the pilot's chair. Finally he shrugged his shoulders and smiled as he walked over to the weapons array.

"You've all gone mad and that's down to you Alienbutt. You're a bad influence." He pointed at the seated Alienbutt. "But let's get started before I see sense."

Using direction thrusters, Alienbutt set off, guiding the ship with minimum power out of the moon's orbit and on a trajectory that would bring them up behind the first of the warships. As they came within range for the torpedoes, Thrumbar fired. As soon as the torpedoes were fired Alienbutt hit the power and shot off towards the second ship. As explosions ripped apart the rear of the first ship, Thrumbar fired the next spread of torpedoes. The enemy warship began to react but it was too slow and the second wave of torpedoes hit home. The second warship suffered the same fate as the first. As the engines began to detonate, the ships disappeared in a chain reaction of explosions. The troop ships started to move, but Alienbutt was already pouncing on the first, with forward lasers firing. The light defences of the troop ships stood no chance against Alienbutt's frigate at such close quarters. Within minutes of the first torpedoes being fired, Alienbutt was heading his ship away from the planet and preparing to jump to light speed, leaving the two war ships as burning hulks, and five of the troop ships afire with fresh explosions ripping through them as more fuel and ammunition exploded.

Admiral Frederick's dreadnought jumped out of light speed, quickly followed by the saviours of his fleet. The main base had been totally destroyed, along with all the dreadnoughts there. Only his patrol of ten ships had survived. While waiting for the probe's report on the attack on their base, they had received news of the invasion of the Ick Empire. Knowing that a superior force was out in space probably searching for them, Frederick had headed for the Big Rocks system so he could hide out in the asteroid belt there. Once there, he could find out what was happening and who he could trust. He was a long way from home with no idea who stood between him and safety, if there would be any safety when they got there.

Soon after reaching their hiding spot, they picked up a coded message on a secure Ick frequency. The message was being relayed through a robotic spy probe and was short, but gave the Admiral a renewed hope. Sending out a scout craft to retrieve the spy probe that had sent the message, Frederick started to make plans.

CHAPTER 13

A New Order.

INTERSTELLAR NEWS CHANNEL 9.
NEWS FLASH

The Federation Senate today released the following statement;

It has been discovered that the troubles of recent years leading to the coffee bean shortage has been down to elements within the Ick Empire who were trying to sabotage the universal peace for their own ends. A planned invasion by rebel Ick fleets to take control of the coffee production planets and thereby control the universe has been thwarted by E.D.F. forces working in support of the new Federation Navy. In large space battles over the last week, the invasion force has been soundly beaten and chased back into Ick space.

The Federation and Coffee houses of Earth, now stand at war with the Ick rebels, who had seized control of the Empire, and until this war is won, all civilian space travel is forbidden unless you have clearance from the E.D.F. and martial law will be called on any planet where unrest starts. It is believed that the rebel Ick were not acting alone but in collusion with members of the Federation. Until those regimes are flushed out these measures will remain to protect us all.

Hydroponic had once been a bounty hunter, one of the very best, and for a while, partner to Blackarachnia. They worked together as the two of them began to build a legend around themselves. But he had walked, or rather flown away from that life and set off to see what there was to see in the universe. He had travelled for more than ten years, and in that time he had seen the Lava falls of Zune and flown through the Trippycolour Nebula at the end of the universe. He had surfed the galactic hurricane winds and searched for the legendary lost empire of Sinai, who held the secret of eternal life. He had searched for every improbable thing that he had ever heard of, and often found they were true. But as he read the latest news reports, he knew without doubt that he was reading bullshit. Never would the Ick do what they had been accused of, while he also knew those who ran the Coffee Houses were total power freaks who wanted to rule the universe; but the Ick would always stand in their way. He was hot on the trail of hunting down the Giant Space Worm of Ulric Dreadlord, a mythical creature not seen in over ten thousand years. Some things, though, are more important than seeing what's over the next hill, and his debt to the murdered Ick leader Wickede was one of those things. Turning his ship around, he plotted a course to take him back. It would take a few months at full speed, but he had found the secret from the Sinai Empire, so time didn't mean much to him anymore, as he had all of eternity. If the Ick still held out or not when he got there it would change nothing. It was time for him to start blowing things up, and the more he thought about it, the more he realised that he missed his old life. He wondered if Blackarachnia would be in the middle of things helping the Ick. He did hope so. It would be good to fly with his old partner again.

Captain Noble had heard the report with disgust; she had seen the official news reports of the invasion of the Ick Empire and also seen the broadcasts by the Ick that the Federation was working hard to block. Those reports showed the mass extermination of the populations of the invaded Ick planets, robot troops firing on civilians. Now all bounty hunters were ordered by the Federation to take up positions along the Ick border with the asteroid belt of Ashia Minor to prevent Ick refugees from escaping the advancing robot army of the Federation, or they would be classed as traitors to the Federation. All fleeing Ick peoples were to be rounded up and placed in camps awaiting processing to find the traitors.

All registered bounty hunters in the Outer Systems had been recalled to the giant space station that was the headquarters of the law enforcement out there. Some of the hunters were new blood who would do any task for the right price, but there were still many of the old school, those who had fought alongside the Ick or just held to principles about not involving civilians in business. She could feel the unrest as the orders were given out, and knew that within the hour she would be contacted by many who would feel as she did. The Ick were being set up and wiped out despite what was said on the news channels. The Federation was trying to hide the facts behind a smoke screen of scare stories about coffee production sabotage.

Duke Ramboe had been commander of the bounty hunter operation in the Outer Systems for almost twenty years. Before that, he had been one of the hunters. He was a huge figure who towered over everyone; no one was sure to which species he belonged, but at over seven feet tall and built like a small mountain, he kept order over the bounty hunters by commanding respect and by brute force on the very odd occasion that it was needed. He had read out the orders from the Federation, delivered to him by a very nervous officer in the uniform of the new Federal Navy. He could feel the unrest building from his hunters. Unlike the hunters from the central systems who never got to chase anything worse than someone who wouldn't pay their taxes, those of the Outer System were independent and fiercely loyal to each other. The Ick had always given the hunters aid over the years as they chased down pirate gangs and other violent individuals. Although the Ick couldn't hold a bounty hunter licence as they were not part of the Federation, they were seen as part of the family by the bounty hunters. For the Federation to prevent the Ick people from escaping a war zone that was wiping them out, just went to show how little those who ran the Federation knew or cared about the Outer Systems. Over three hundred hunters were gathered aboard the station so far and they had been given two hours to sign up for this mission.

Upon Duke Ramboe's return to his office, he ordered his ship prepped for flight and sent a message for Captain Noble and Jack Lantern to come see him. As two of the more experienced hunters he would be able to confirm his feel for the mood and which way most would lean if asked. Looking out of his view screen, he saw the six battle cruisers of the Federal Navy sitting off from the space station. Studying the ships, he noted the design and shape. You could see the influence of the Ick dreadnought in their design but these were larger and reportedly packed a lot more fire power, but still they had that Ick look to them. He had heard rumours that the Ick were building a replacement for the dreadnought and he wondered if they would have been much like these Federal battle cruisers.

A new order had just been created in the universe. The Federation, set up thousands of years before to foster trade and peace through mutual respect and co-operation, had now turned to the use of force and threats to protect the very thing that was causing the problem. The universal addiction to coffee had made everyone a slave to the Coffee Houses and the crop they produced, and now even the Federation Senate had fallen to their plans and plots. Duke Ramboe may have been sitting on a space station light years from the Inner Systems and their politics, but he had a network of friends and agents to rival any intelligence service. He knew who would support the Coffee Houses, wanting to increase their own power, and who, if they could create the right conditions, would support the old order and work to bring about a return of that order. He had read the Book of Ick and the one followed by the other side and knew that everything depended on a dead Ick leader and the last of the Alienbutts finding a cure to the coffee bean addiction. If information was power, then he was one of the most powerful people in the known universe and he now had to convince his hunters to risk their lives for a plan that he wasn't sure would work.

More than half the Empire had been overrun within a few days. The High Council had either been captured or killed when the Ick home world had been attacked within hours of the naval central command falling. As the empire's population got aboard anything that would fly to escape the approaching fleets of the Federal Navies, Snoodgrass planned the defence of what was left of the empire. Alienbutt had again proved why Wickede had placed so much faith in him, showing how to cancel out the battle cruisers' superior fire power, and he now worked with Commander Grommit on working out battle tactics. The surviving Ick Navy had started to slow down the advance of the invasion and in a number of small skirmishes had made the advancing battle cruisers retreat. Without realising it, Alienbutt had become a commander of the Ick forces. Leading raiding forces to protect civilian fleets that were fleeing, or by just being a badly-dressed drunken oaf, he lifted the spirits of the Ick forces. The Ick began to tell and retell stories of his exploits which expanded with every telling. Many called for him to be made a Defender of the Empire, an honour not bestowed in over four hundred years, and never to a non Ick. Yet Snoodgrass noticed a change in Alienbutt's manner. He was more business-like and cold; there was an edge to him now that he hoped he would never see. In front of everyone he acted like Alienbutt, the funny drunken bounty hunter they had come to know, but he saw the worried glances from Killashandra. But with so much else to worry about, he didn't have time to speak to his friend. He would have to hope that Alienbutt had the strength of character to ride the wave and not be swamped by the dark events happening.

So far Snoodgrass had held the Fo'c'sle in reserve, knowing he would need them as it was only a matter of time before the two forces would meet again in a large battle. Transferred from the dreadnoughts to the more agile frigates that Alienbutt flew, he had also had Grommit choose their best fifty fighter pilots to be trained to fly those ships. He had now split the Fo'c'sle into three squadrons under the command of Grommit, Cyborgpirate and Killashandra. A fourth squadron of the frigates would be commanded by Alienbutt with crews from the Ick Navy. From the reports that he was receiving, he knew the enemy was massing a fleet of over three thousand of their battle cruisers, ready for a final attack on the Ick. They would be heavily outnumbered, having less than a thousand dreadnoughts and just the four squadrons of frigates, but he had a number of new experimental weapons that he hoped would give them an edge.

A priest in an orange cassock from the Order of Ick walked into his office. Snoodgrass looked over hopefully but the priest shook his head.

"The book is revealing nothing. We have found a passage telling of the loss of Wickede, it is now in plain sight and obvious, but it will reveal nothing more. It is often thought by those who study the Book that it only reveals its secrets at the appointed time."

"You speak as if the Book is alive and conscious of events that are happening to us," said Snoodgrass in disgust. He knew the theory the priest spoke of, but had hoped for just a hint he was on the right track.

"That has been said many times before, Snoodgrass, the Book is a guide. It will point us in the right direction at times and confirm decisions made, but it will not tell us what to do. The Omniverse does not work in such a manner."

"So when we need an edge, the Book has decided to keep quiet," said Snoodgrass, slumping back in his chair, rubbing his tired eyes. It had been a few days since he had last slept for even a couple of hours and his usually sharp mind was starting to get fuzzy as the weight of responsibility bore down on him.

"You need some sleep, and I don't need the Book to tell me that. What good will you be to your people if you collapse from exhaustion?" Alienbutt said from the doorway. Neither the priest nor Snoodgrass had noticed him arrive. He walked over to a chair and sat down, placing an unopened bottle of whiskey on the table. He still wore his ridiculous lucky boots and Blackarachnia's coat but now had found a bejewelled codpiece that would be blinding if you shined a light onto it. The leather kilt had been replaced by deep purple velvet leggings and a chain mail vest dyed black. To anyone who didn't know him when he had left Sloppystool with Blackarachnia, his outlandish dress sense was just part of him. To Snoodgrass and the others he still looked comical.

"Admiral Frederick just sent a message; he lost most of his command but is hoping to break through the blockade surrounding the empire's space by going through Ashia Minor," said Snoodgrass, accepting a drink offered by Alienbutt. "When he arrives he can help take some of the weight off my shoulders, until then I don't have time to sleep."

CHAPTER 14

Plans and Plots.

INTERSTELLAR NEWS CHANNEL 9.
NEWS FLASH

The new Federation Navy is reporting smashing victories against the Ick rebel forces, who are in total rout. The Ick home world has already been liberated and the rebels who had been plotting against the Federation and the Coffee Houses have mainly been captured or killed. The newly appointed Ick Emperor Brickcodee, cousin of the murdered Wickede, who had been taken prisoner just after his coronation, has praised the swift action that released him and is helping to bring justice to his cousin's killers.

The last of the Ick rebel leaders, Admiral Frederick and Snoodgrass, the treacherous advisor to the late Wickede, are now rallying their rebel forces for a final battle.

The Ick leaders sat in the makeshift war room, waiting on Snoodgrass. They knew why the meeting had been called; the Federation fleet was reported to be on the move. Snoodgrass entered with Admiral Frederick and walked to the head of the table. The Admiral had finally arrived the day before, and had been sat locked away with Snoodgrass since then. Around the table sat Alienbutt, the three Fo'c'sle commanders and four officers from the Ick Navy who would command the dreadnoughts and Ick fighter pilots. All had been briefed on the Federation battle cruisers' weaknesses and had been training their commands to take advantage of this.

"I will make this as brief as possible," stated Snoodgrass. "Admiral Frederick will take command of the Ick fleet, while Grommit commands the frigate squadrons. We have chosen the Dagnabbit System to make our stand and for the last few days we have been laying plasma mines in strategic locations to prevent our enemy flanking us. Our job is simple; we have to stop them here or everything is lost. There can be no retreat or second chances; we don't have the luxury of a plan B. The Federation cannot throw their full force at us as they need to control everywhere else. Not all the Federation are happy with the turn of events, and until the new regime are secure in themselves, they need to use their new-found power to intimidate any elements that may cause problems. If we can stop them at Dagnabbit then we stand a good chance of others joining our cause. We have a few surprises, and if we can hit them hard and hurt them at the outset of the battle, then keep them off balance, we have a chance. Much will depend on how disciplined their force is. We have to hope they will freeze when they come face to face with true Ick resistance."

He didn't need to state what would happen if they lost, as they were all fully aware that the future of the Ick people depended on them at the very least holding out for a draw.

Hundreds of thousands of Ick refugees had come to the Dagnabbit system hoping to find protection, and if the battle went badly they would be at the mercy of the Federation forces.

As the Ick leaders began to disperse after the briefing, Admiral Frederick came up to Alienbutt and took him to one side.

"Alienbutt, have you ever heard of F.T.L.?"

Piestoff shook his head. "No. Should I have? What is it?"

"I was hoping you would tell me. We found a spy probe out near Crazy Robot. It seems it picked up a faint signal with Wickede's call sign attached. It said to send Alienbutt, F.T.L. working." Frederick tried to hide the disappointment he felt. He was hoping that Alienbutt would understand the message and somehow know what to do, as stated in his role in the Book of Ick.

"Sorry, no idea what it could mean, Admiral. Maybe Snoodgrass may have an idea."

Frederick shrugged his shoulders. "Probably an old message drifting around. You sometimes get ghost messages out there, they echo around for decades." Frederick may have been a convert to the Book, but he was also a practical person. It had been a faint hope at best but now he had other things to think about. Snoodgrass's plan for the coming battle was dependent on far too much luck and things that might not happen, but they didn't have another option open to them. After the battle he would ask Snoodgrass. For the moment they all had too much to worry about.

The bounty hunters set off from the space station the next day, there was over two hundred ships of various design, from small deep space frigates to larger war ships or converted trading vessels. It was a mismatched fleet of ships, flown in no order or formation but piloted by some of the best fighters in the universe. With them went a supporting fleet of thirty Federation battle cruisers moving in tight formation, looking much more deadly to the untrained eye. They headed for the border of Ick space where any fleeing Ick vessel would cross out of Ick space. Duke Ramboe had personally arrested twenty hunters at gunpoint who had refused to join the fleet heading out. Now he held them in custody awaiting transfer by prison ship. Amongst them was Captain Noble. The fleet would be in position within a day's time and the Federation commander had informed Duke Ramboe that the first of the fleeing Ick ships was expected within forty eight hours as the final offensive against the remnants of the Ick began. Jack Lantern was appointed to relay orders from the Federation fleet to the bounty hunters, and picked up a local guide to help pinpoint the area of space most likely for the Ick to use for their escape route.

Jack Lantern stood in the office of the Federation flagship, the guide organising the plans for the operation stood with three officers.

"The Ick have heavily mined large areas of space along this frontier to prevent pirate raids on their outlying colonies, so there is only one real route they can take," pointed out the guide, indicating a small area of space on the holo map. "The small ships of the bounty hunters can hide just inside the asteroid field and not be detected by the Ick sensor sweeps, but these great beasts," he indicated the ship he stood on, "will have to hide further inside the field."

"Where do you suggest? Remember we need to move fast when the Ick arrive," asked one of the officers. He was a fresh-faced officer, probably on his first tour. The guide typed some coordinates into the map control panel that highlighted an area before them on the map.

"Here is a clear space within the Asteroids, only a short way in but your ships would be invisible. There is a clear channel through the floating rocks to there, so using your onboard computers you can fly in at speed and avoid being seen by anyone watching. There's plenty of room in there for a fleet twice the size of this one."

The Federation officers looked over the guide's plans on the map screen, and then the most senior turned and spoke.

"What of the pockets of dead space dotted around this area?"

The guide took a deep breath, clearly shocked at the officer's knowledge of the area. "There are areas to both sides about four to five light years away, but that area is the product of the Ick mining in the asteroid field a thousand or so years ago. They needed a clear way in for those great big strip mining ships to get to the deposits. Now it's the perfect place for you to hide in."

The officer looked satisfied at the explanation and finally he nodded his approval. He knew he was inexperienced to be leading such a large fleet, having only served as an inner system escort commander and never seen true active service, but the Federation was short of officers for its new navy. As a result he was going to be smart enough to follow the lead set down by the local experts so he would not end up looking stupid. Asking the odd question and knowing a little local knowledge would make him appear more experienced, he hoped.

"Return to your ship, Lantern, we set off at once. Ensure your hunters are in position and ready. I don't want anyone spying our fleet and tipping off the Ick."

Jack Lantern nodded. "Just ensure we get the rest of the credits promised as that's all we're interested in. This is your war, not ours."

With that he turned and left, the guide a step behind.

Glenn Scrimshaw

Neither said a word until they were aboard Jack's ship.

"I hope you know what you're doing, Lantern. If this goes wrong we got thirty of those monsters on our back," the guide said, clearly worried. Jack gave a cold smile.

"They're inexperienced fools. You thought fast on your feet there with the Ick mining story. They will zoom in to where you said and be in the middle of dead space before they know it. Relax, Ruck, you worry too much. That officer was so green if you had told him to hit the self-destruct button he would have."

They both watched as the battle cruisers sped away, heading for the area indicated by Ruck to enter the asteroid belt of Ashia Minor. When the last of the ships entered the asteroid belt Jack ordered one of the hunters, Neon Rogue, to follow them to ensure they ended up trapped in dead space. As he watched the small hunter's ship head off to follow, he sent a message back to Duke Ramboe who should have set off from the space station with Captain Noble and the rest of the hunters. All being well, the Federation fleet should be stuck in dead space, and the next part of their plan could begin. In any event Neon Rogue would have reported back by the time Ramboe got here and revealed the next step of the plan to help the Ick.

Geurick Tackful had worked for the Coffee Houses since he was a young boy. Handpicked by the Order of SpaceMasons to be taught the secrets of the Book, he had excelled and became the youngest of their hunters, the military arm of the order, in its history. Now he was their best active hunter, but even he was surprised when he got the summons for a personal meeting with the President of the Grand Order of the Bean, the organisation behind the Coffee Houses. The security surrounding the location of the meeting had been tight. Only a handful of people knew the true identity of their leader so as Geurick was ushered into the darkened room he felt apprehension for the first time in many years. Ahead of him he could just make out the shadowy form of a man sat behind a large table, so he concentrated on his other senses. He could smell the rich aroma of coffee, but behind that smell an almost cheesy smell. From outside the room no noise filtered in and the only light was from a dim lamp off to his left.

"You are the hunter." It wasn't a question needing a reply but a statement. Geurick picked out slight movement and heard the crunching of someone eating. "We have received a transmission offering us the whereabouts of Blackarachnia and Nifty the Niffler in return for certain equipment. We believe this to be a fair trade and wish for it to proceed without any problems. When you leave here you will be given the details of the trade with this new player, a being using the name of Mr. Fluffy. Your task is to find the two traitors and bring them in to our custody or destroy them. Mr. Fluffy may prove useful again, so he is to be given what he asks for."

Geurick could have jumped for joy, but settled for a slight smile; finally he was being given the chance to test his skills against Blackarachnia. Soon he would show that it was he and not the bounty hunter who was the most deadly in the universe. His entire career was put in the shade by the bounty hunter. It was Blackarachnia who got the accolades and respect while Geurick was in his shadow, always seen as second best. Now he could prove who the better killer was.

As he turned to leave the room he pinpointed the cheesy smell. It was the smell of the cheesy snack known as cheese puffs. Not sure what to make of that he put his discovery to one side, too eager to begin his planning to kill Blackarachnia.

CHAPTER 15

Dagnabbit or Bust.

INTERSTELLAR NEWS CHANNEL 9.
NEWS FLASH

The Federation Navy are expected to announce victory over the rebel Ick forces later today as they deploy a superior fleet against the remnants of the forces hiding in the Dagnabbit System. After a string of smashing victories the mood amongst the Federation forces is high and they do not foresee any problems mopping up the last of the traitors. The Federal Navy has the most advanced ships ever assembled and the robotic support units will ensure that the loss of life will be kept to a minimum amongst the crews. Once victory is achieved it is expected that the navies will concentrate on protecting the trade routes and help bring about a golden age of peace to the universe.

Alienbutt sat in the pilot's chair of his frigate. Behind him was arrayed a squadron of thirty frigates that he still couldn't understand how he had become commander of. To his left were the squadrons of Killashandra, Grommit and Cyborgpirate, a total of one hundred and twenty ships that would be the first to meet the advancing Federation fleet. Each of the new Fo'c'sle squadrons had painted emblems onto their ships' hulls to identify which squadron they now belonged to. Cyborgpirate's had adopted a skull and crossbones while Grommit's had chosen a large black cross. Killashandra's ships were all adorned with a tartan thistle. Much to Alienbutt's embarrassment, the Ick under his command had chosen a flaming kebab on a green shield as their emblem.

Their battle plans were simple; they were to stay hidden and allow the advancing fleet to pass them by and then hit them from behind as they entered the Dagnabbit System. Their best reports said the enemy fleet numbered around two thousand five hundred of the battle cruisers and around another thousand troop and support vessels. They had orders to stay behind the advancing fleet as Snoodgrass had some surprises waiting before he would launch the dreadnoughts and Ick fighters, and he didn't want the Fo'c'sle to spoil them.

They had been sitting for a few hours waiting for the signal to start the attack run, so Alienbutt had ordered half a dozen bottles of whiskey to be placed next to his chair, and sat absently sipping them, the result of which made him hungry, so he ordered a couple of large kebabs brought up from the kitchen. As a crew member carried the kebabs over to him the closed circuit fleet radio crackled to life.

"O.K. everyone, let's get ready. The Federation fleet is entering the target area."

Alienbutt shook his head in disbelief and then swore. He opened up the communication to reply to Grommit.

"Look Grommit, can you give us at least ten minutes, my kebabs have just arrived." He took the plate and thanked the crew member for bringing them with a nod.

"Alienbutt! Let me get this right, we're about to fight the largest space battle in history and you're asking us to put it on hold so you can eat your kebabs? Just let me ask the Federation to stop for a bit or if they could reschedule for tomorrow maybe?" Grommit's voice was caught half way between outrage and amusement, but then other voices came over the radio giving their support to allow the kebabs to be eaten first. Grommit smiled to herself. Without even realising it Alienbutt had broken the tension that had been building as they had watched the massive Federation fleet go past. The Fo'c'sle was the best, but even so the tension of waiting would be telling.

"You've got two minutes for the kebabs, Alienbutt and another one minute to finish off that whiskey I know you're drinking. Now let's have some order, we're supposed to be professionals," Grommit replied, trying to sound serious.

"I've got a spare kebab if you want to nip over, Grommit. I'll even light a few candles and make it all romantic, and promise not to tell anyone if you can't resist my charms and snog me again."

Grommit's response was short, abusive and drowned out half way through by cheers and lewd comments that came over the radio.

The Federation fleet spread for miles as it moved closer to the Dagnabbit System, their ships travelling in fixed formations with the battle cruisers boxing in the lighter defences of the robot troop ships and other support vessels. Robot fighters darted between the capital ships, looking like flies swarming between giant animals. They flew through Ick space, confident of victory because of their overwhelming numbers and greater fire power. The Fo'c'sle approached from above and behind at great speed. These were the finest fighting units in the universe, each confident of their superior skills and experience and knowing they would take down the enemy in great numbers. They may be massively outnumbered, but for them, numbers just meant more targets to blow up. The enemy fleet moved along like some giant herd, tightly packed and slow. It was time for the hunters to spring.

As the back markers of the enemy fleet started to react to the approaching Fo'c'sle, Grommit gave the order to open fire and hundreds of torpedoes were fired in wave after wave to impact on the rear of the enemy fleet before the frigates of the Fo'c'sle swung away. The torpedoes were guided by computerised guidance systems and had shield scrambling emitters so they could pass through any energy shield. They pinpointed the great battle cruisers' weaknesses and the explosions were so intense that a shock wave raced out like an earthquake, buffeting ships and causing even more chaos and collisions amongst the tightly packed ships. The Fo'c'sle outran the worst of the effects of the shock wave but as it passed them by, slightly buffeting their ships, they slowed and turned back to the Federation fleet. With menacing slowness they re-formed, ready to strike again.

"This is Grommit to all squadrons, prepare for another assault, then we split and choose our targets. Happy hunting and drinks are on that fat-arsed Alienbutt if I don't end up shooting him down myself. We kill 'em all."

Alienbutt grinned and threw an empty whiskey bottle over his shoulder before grabbing a fresh one. A calm had settled over him that he only seemed to achieve in combat, no nerves or doubt, just a clarity of thought. While waiting for the action to start he had been nervous and his butt plugs had been tested, but now the battle had started, he didn't need them, but just in case, he kept them in as the rest of the crew wouldn't be much use if they were knocked out by an accidental gas leak.

The frigates formed ranks like old style cavalry, for a second charge as the Federation battle cruisers tried to break free of formation and the wreckage of burning ships to turn to meet the next attack. Over three hundred ships blazed and others were still suffering as continued explosions from the first attack ripped at them, and already the fast, agile frigates were starting their second attack run and firing a new wave of torpedoes. But this time the Federation fleet returned fire as the first of the battle cruisers moved into position to defend the fleet. The destruction this time was far less, as many of the Federation ships had prepared for the second strike, but still more ships exploded as torpedoes found their targets. The Fo'c'sle ships this time didn't peel off their attack run but entered the tightly packed Federation fleet's formation, choosing targets at will. The larger Federation ships, unable to manoeuvre in such a tight formation, became sitting ducks as their engines were targeted and the ships crippled. The Federation robot fighters began to stream out of hangar bays to defend against the attack, but were no match for the flying skills of the Fo'c'sle pilots unless they could gather in more numbers and try to swarm over them. As the enemy fleet continued to advance, it was leaving a trail of damaged and destroyed ships as the Fo'c'sle vented their anger at being held back from combat, wanting to defend and avenge the people who had taken them in and given them a home. The Federation had invaded Ick space and now they would ensure that there was some payback.

Just as the robot fighters began to gather in enough numbers to cause a problem, they received the order to withdraw and grudgingly began pulling away from the Federation fleet. They raced back along the advancing fleet's flight path, passing the hundreds of ships they had crippled and destroyed. They had caused heavy damage and their losses were light but the Federation fleet flew onwards and all knew the damage wasn't enough to stop the enemy fleet. It was time for the second part of Snoodgrass's plan.

Snoodgrass stood on the flight deck of the command centre watching the Fo'c'sle fleet's attack on a giant holo-screen. Ahead of the approaching fleet was the first of his surprises; millions of a new design plasma mine had been placed in the advancing fleet's flight path. The system of Dagnabbit was home to a secret research facility for new Ick weapons and Snoodgrass had put a few of the better ideas into mass production. As the Federation ships moved into the minefield, those mines that made contact with the ships stuck magnetically to the hulls. As each one did, it sent a tiny signal so the Ick would know what percentage of them had found targets.

The first wave of ships to enter became covered with hundreds of the small mines. While the explosive force of them was relatively small, it was the number of mines attached that would do the damage. As the fleet reached a pre-arranged point, the order was sent for the Fo'c'sle to disengage. As the frigates turned and retreated, Snoodgrass ordered the mines to be detonated. The entire front ranks of the Federation fleet disappeared in a massive explosion. The shields designed to prevent phaser and torpedo attack proved useless against the small magnetic mines that blew hundreds of small holes in the ships' hulls, causing them to crumple as the pressure of escaping air into space tore larger sections of the hull apart. The Federation fleet stuttered as hundreds of ships were totally ripped apart, while others were badly damaged. The Ick commander smiled grimly, then sent in his next surprise.

Twenty dreadnoughts had been refitted to each carry a large ion cannon. The ion cannon was the most devastating weapon ever created, sending a concentrated beam of magnetic energy that would rip apart whatever it hit. But it was unpredictable and prone to self-destruct if it didn't have a planet to earth itself with, as with the one they had encountered in the Big Rocks System. The ships, crewed by volunteers in case of this malfunction, opened fire into the now panicking Federation fleet, each deadly blast ripping through the ships' shields, delivering devastating damage. As the new round of carnage continued, the order for the full fleet to attack was given. Admiral Frederick led the Ick dreadnoughts and their fighters forward to attack and the Fo'c'sle fleet again swung around and started another attack run.

The Federation fleet began to break apart, as the inexperienced captains started to panic. Most of the crews were in their first real battle against an organised force and the massive damage that had suddenly happened to the forefront of their fleet formation had unnerved many. In their rush to try and avoid the advancing Ick fleet, many collisions occurred as the battle cruisers tried to manoeuvre to break free of the tight formation that they were in.

Admiral Frederick, at the head of fifty dreadnoughts, punched a hole towards the centre of the Federation fleet, seeking to destroy the troop and support ships, while the Fo'c'sle separated into their squadrons again and started to hit at any available target. When the first of the dreadnoughts with the ion cannons self-destructed, Snoodgrass ordered them to disengage and fall back. The large cannons were still in the experimental stage and being used for the first time. The damage had been done, and now the Ick fleet had engaged the enemy, targets for the cannons were more difficult to choose.

Killashandra sat at the weapons console picking targets with deadly accuracy, while she was a promising pilot, Grommit had decided to place a more experienced pilot at the ship's controls, not wanting to risk losing one of her commanders to inexperience. This didn't bother Killashandra as she felt the need to be blowing things up. Alienbutt had told her what had happened to her friends from the Ladies' Darts Team. She still struggled to believe that her childhood friends were gone, but she was determined that the Federation would pay, and blowing things up seemed to help release the rage that had been threatening to overwhelm her. In the strange pilot Ponnfarr, who had been Kali's lead fighter pilot before she was injured, she had someone who was totally fearless when put in a battle situation, but he seemed more than a little crazy. He had started laughing as the Fo'c'sle had started their first attack run and had become more maniacal as the battle progressed; even now she could hear him giggling to himself. Despite his odd behaviour he flew the ship with great skill and seemed totally aware of everything going on around them. Time and again he would close in on an enemy ship and every time he would give Killashandra the perfect shot at the cruiser's weak spot. Their frigate flew between the massive battle cruisers with her squadron following, explosions ripping apart ships all around them as torpedoes found their targets. The smaller forward laser cannons helped clear away the robot fighters that were now around in large numbers trying to stop their enemies. In the confusion of the battle, pilots had to be aware of danger coming from any angle as ships dived from above or rose from below, trying to destroy the enemy in a massive free-for-all. The battle cruisers that were so effective when their targets were at a distance were proving ineffective at such close quarters and their pilots' lack of real battle experience now became a death sentence for their crews.

Cyborgpirate piloted his ship with a concentration heightened by a cold psychotic rage that always descended when he engaged in battle. Any thought of organising the combat was impossible. He knew you just had to keep moving and shooting and pray that today wasn't your day. Following his ship was his wingman of many years, Elxa Rowce, as they flew along under a battle cruiser, it began to list drastically. Cyborgpirate put his ship into a dive as the cruiser dipped further, but was unable to prevent his ship colliding, causing a hole to be ripped down his hull and smashing the left wing of his frigate. Out of control, the Fo'c'sle commander spun away and down through the battle. Elxa had no time to watch Cyborgpirate's fate as he too tried to take action to avoid the crippled cruiser as it dropped into his flight path. Unable to do anything else he gave a curse a second before his ship hit the cruiser and exploded. Two other Fo'c'sle frigates sped after Cyborgpirate's crippled ship as it fell through the battle, trying to provide cover for their commander from any robot fighter that would see the damaged ship as an easy target to attack, hoping that their commander was still alive and they could keep him that way.

Alienbutt flew through the battlefield, still taking sips from a bottle of whiskey as he manoeuvred around burning hulks to find ever more targets. He was aware that very soon they would run out of torpedoes and be left with just their forward cannons. The battle formation of the Federation was starting to break apart as already some of their ships were starting to run. Ahead of him, he saw a number of battle cruisers begin to form up into a fighting wedge, moving forward with purpose to engage the Ick dreadnoughts. Any wrecks in their path were blasted out of the way. Ordering his squadron to rally on him he set off towards the threat. Only seventeen ships of his squadron answered the call, but all quickly formed up behind him as they started an attack run to hit the battle cruisers from behind. They only had the one run at the ships, but their torpedoes found their mark and the fighting wedge fell apart, before the remaining ships were targeted by the Ick dreadnoughts that had also responded to the threat of the organised group.

Snoodgrass stood watching the battle unfold; he knew that the Federation fleet was ready to bolt. If he had reserves, this would be the moment he would send them in. Then a fleet jumped out of light speed, high above the main battle. Snoodgrass stared at the holo-screen in panic at the new arrivals; the battle wasn't won yet. But then he grinned as he recognised the ships as they took up formation beyond the edge of the battle.

"Snoodgrass you old dog, I'm hurt you didn't invite me, but I brought my lads and lasses to gatecrash your little battle anyway, as I'm sure our missing invite was an oversight on your part," boomed Duke Ramboe's voice over the radio. Snoodgrass shook his head and chuckled.

"I'm sure I sent you an invitation Duke, but feel free to join in," replied Snoodgrass, grinning in spite of himself, knowing now the battle was won.

The bounty hunter fleet began to move, dropping like a bolt of lightning onto the centre of the Federation fleet where the enemy command ship was. Duke Ramboe's ship was at the forefront of the attack and he ordered all ships to fire on the Federation command vessel, and within moments it disappeared in a giant explosion. All Federation resistance crumbled with the loss of the Federation Admiral and the battle quickly became a rout. The battle cruisers started to retreat and left the slower troop ships, support vessels and other damaged ships to their own fate, which had become very short and ended in large explosions, as the Ick were in no mood for giving quarter after what had happened to the populations of the planets that had been overrun by the invaders.

Grommit flew clear of the battlefield, climbing high above the burning wrecks that floated lifeless. Behind her followed the remains of her squadron. Their losses had been heavy, but not as bad as expected. Two miles above the last of the wrecks, she levelled off and finally looked down over the scene of the battle. Never had she seen such carnage. Below her thousands of ships burnt, and still the Ick forces swept through the area finding and finishing off damaged Federation ships. The Federation armada had numbered thousands of ships; at least two-thirds of which were now reduced to burning scrap metal. The battle had been short but fierce. Snoodgrass's little surprises had made the difference. The shock at the destruction of the front ranks of their fleet where most of the more experienced captains had been was too much for them to recover from in such a short period of time.

The Ick were inventors of gadgets that excelled in going bang. She couldn't understand why they didn't rule space, but were content to stay within their own empire's border. This stance was now seeing them face a war of extinction. She had no illusions that they had won anything more than a battle, and that the Federation would come back stronger once they had nursed their wounds. Now was the time they should be counter-attacking but they just didn't have the forces, even with the arrival of the bounty hunters under the leadership of the legendary Duke Ramboe. They would have to dig in and build up their defences, and await the next move against them, unless they got more help.

CHAPTER 16

A Quest Revealed.

INTERSTELLAR NEWS CHANNEL 9.
NEWS FLASH

As news continues to come in of a defeat for the Federation's new navy in the Dagnabbit System, the role of the Senate has been called into question during this time of war. The new Senate Security Council has implemented new powers so they can better wage the war against the Ick traitors and their allies. The Security Council will now have direct control over security issues while the Senate deal with the day to day running of the Federation. The Coffee Houses have been granted two representatives on the Security Council so that distribution of the bean can better be implemented and protected. The new ten-strong Council are expected to announce new measures to prevent the escalation of hostilities, as some outlying systems show signs of showing limited support for the Ick rebels.

In the aftermath of the battle, more refugees flooded into the Dagnabbit system to take refuge, protected by the last of the Ick Navy. All who were able were set to work salvaging anything usable from the battlefield, as most of the main production facilities had been destroyed to prevent them being captured as the enemy had overrun them. The Federation had retreated back to the edge of Ick space as they had lost almost all their robotic forces and over half their battle cruisers. Now they seemed content to blockade Ick space while they awaited fresh orders. The only route into Ick space was through Ashia Minor which was being held open by Duke Ramboe and his bounty hunters, aided by Cyborgpirate, who had been found alive in the wreckage of his ship, and Killashandra's Fo'c'sle squadrons. Here regular skirmishes would take place as resources were smuggled to the Ick.

Almost two weeks after the battle, Alienbutt returned to Dagnabbit after patrolling the borders of Ick controlled space, and received a request to see Snoodgrass. After ensuring his squadron had all docked and the crews were billeted, Alienbutt headed over to the command station where Snoodgrass was based. He used one of the little runarounds that acted as shuttles around the makeshift encampment above the planet. Alienbutt noticed that Admiral Frederick's dreadnought was also docked at the command station. As soon as he docked, he was escorted up to Snoodgrass's private office. As he entered the room, Snoodgrass jumped up from his chair, grinning.

"At last, Piestoff. I was starting to think you would never get back."

"We ran into a Federation patrol as we started back, so had to convince them to bugger off back to where they came from," replied Alienbutt as he wandered over to where Frederick held a bottle of whiskey out for him.

"Wickede is alive!" Snoodgrass continued excitedly. "He

managed to engage the F.T.L. drive just before the torpedoes hit his ship."

Piestoff fumbled the bottle of whiskey, almost dropping it. Recovering his grip on the bottle he took a long drink, and then stared at the two grinning Ick commanders.

"Let me sit down and then explain what you're on about, and what the hell is a F.T.L. drive?" said a shocked Piestoff, already heading for the nearest chair. How could his friend be alive?

All three sat down and Snoodgrass tried to get a grip on his excitement but failed.

"Frederick picked up one of our spy probes out in the Outer System that intercepted a message from Wickede. Send Alienbutt, F.T.L. working. Only myself, Wickede and a rather bizarre scientist who was aboard Wickede's ship with him know of the F.T.L. drive. The message is from Wickede and he needs you to get him back."

Piestoff looked at the two commanders and took another long drink from the whiskey bottle before responding.

"Why did he ask for me in particular? Why not ask for any other ship and captain?"

"Since the battle, the Book of Ick has revealed some more information to us. Using that and information from the spy probe, we have been able to work out roughly where Wickede is. The problem is, a conventional ship can't reach him. We need you to pilot a ship equipped with an F.T.L. drive to bring him back."

"What the hell is an F.T.L. drive, Snoodgrass, and how did Wickede end up so far out?" asked Piestoff, already knowing he wouldn't like the answer. Snoodgrass took a deep breath and finally managed to partly get a grip on his excitement and stop grinning like an idiot.

"The F.T.L. drive was invented by a scientist working for us,

Frank T. L. It's a revolutionary new propulsion system which Wickede was testing when we were ambushed. I've got his research, and now we are building one for the rescue mission. It works by somehow folding and shrinking space and then flying through the middle of it, covering vast distances in seconds. It works on a similar premise to his Hyper Jump, but rather than just transporting people or organic matter over the vast distances of space it can move whole ships, or so we think." Snoodgrass said the last part with uncertainty. "We're not totally sure how it works, to be honest, but we can build one."

"Look Alienbutt, Snoodgrass has had the finest brains we have left working on this and they are baffled by the Professor's work. All we know is it worked for Wickede, but now he's stuck God knows where, and only you have a chance of getting him back. The ship will be ready within a couple of days. We have the co-ordinates and we need you to fly it and..." Frederick paused, looking embarrassed, then he finished, "provide the fuel booster."

Piestoff looked confused, and then Snoodgrass told him of the fuel additive needed to make the drive work. In a universe where strange and stupid things kept happening to him, Alienbutt had just found a new number one strange and stupid thing to crown his life so far. No wonder he drank so much, he thought. His entire people and home world had been destroyed by the ramblings of two mad men thousands of years before. All that to prevent Piestoff from farting while connected to a ship's engines, designed by a mad scientist, to save the leader of the Ick and find a cure for coffee addiction. Either the whole universe was totally insane, or he was so crazy that he needed locking up for his own protection.

Piestoff drained what was left of the whiskey, then got up and walked over to where Snoodgrass kept the drinks and drained another bottle as the two Ick leaders watched in silence.

"I'll be in my quarters until the ship's ready." With that he walked out. The two leaders sat and looked at each other.

"He took it quite well, didn't he?" asked Frederick.

"He only drank two of the three bottles of whiskey I had in my office so I tend to agree," replied Snoodgrass.

Alienbutt had been escorted under guard back to the room that had been turned over for his use late last night; it was two days since he had been told of the plan to rescue Wickede. The room was small, messy and full of empty whiskey bottles. Frederick stood in the doorway surveying the result of Alienbutt's epic bender. On the bed, Alienbutt lay on his back snoring, just wearing one red boot and a pair of tiger print underpants that should have been banned for their skimpiness if nothing else. Frederick stepped into the room, carefully avoiding a discarded kebab, and walked over to the sleeping Alienbutt. Outside the door, two security officers stood waiting, both showing bruises from where they had been hit while trying to subdue the drunken commander the previous night, after the barman in the bar where he was drinking had refused to serve him any more whiskey. Alienbutt's face was also bruised with one eye swollen shut. On his chest were faint marks left from where he had been tazered into submission after he had knocked out the third security officer by hitting him with a chair. Looking down at the unconscious figure to ensure he was not seriously injured, he turned to leave.

"When I was young, back on Sloopystool, me and Nifty once climbed over the wall into the gardens behind the Temple of Sung the one eyed Llama," Alienbutt croaked from a dry throat. "It was a magical place for us; there was a real grass lawn and all these great beautiful plants that were covered in flowers. It even had a pond with a waterfall and real fish swimming. I always wanted a house with a garden."

Frederick turned back towards Alienbutt and looked down at him. Alienbutt lay staring at the ceiling.

"Maybe when this is all over we could sort it out for you," he replied softly.

"They would have to be artificial plants though. I'm no good at keeping plants but with artificial ones it would always look perfect." Alienbutt sat up and swung his feet off the bed. "I liked that old monk from the temple. When he caught us, rather than giving us both a good thrashing, he fed us and told us the story of Sung the one eyed Llama and how he passed on the words of their God through his disciples until someone assassinated him by shooting him from his blind side. That's why they said he was Sung the one eyed Llama, screwed after being shot from the left."

Frederick walked over to a small wash basin and, unable to find a glass, filled an empty whiskey bottle with water.

"You need to sober up, Alienbutt, the ship will be ready soon."

Alienbutt took the offered bottle and drank deeply.

"I think I'm starting to understand how the llama must have felt, a big stupid animal set up before those big crowds; not understanding what the hell's happening but waiting for a bullet."

"You don't believe it was chosen by the Gods then?" asked Frederick.

"The monk told us it was a big con trick but it meant the disciples and monks always had full bellies and a good roof over their heads. People want to believe. The stranger you make it, the more they believe it's true," replied Alienbutt with a half-smile. "And the monk knew, as it was his grandfather's con to start with. He even ordered the animal shot. By making the animal a martyr it made people believe even more, as then it was immortal."

Frederick looked at Alienbutt and saw the terror written on his face, then just as quickly it was gone as Alienbutt smiled.

"Get me a fresh bottle and I'll find my other boot and I'm ready to go." He looked down at himself and noticed his state of undress. "Maybe I should find some clothes too."

Wickede sat on the floor of the ship; the engines and Frank's propulsion drive were burnt out beyond even his ability to repair with the limited tools to hand. To avoid the torpedoes, Frank had used the drive blind and the jump as the drive took over had almost ripped the ship apart. They had no idea where they had ended up, but they were still alive. Using the last of the fuel and basic thrusters, Wickede had managed to get them to a planet near to where they had ended their jump so at least they were not marooned in space. Instead they were marooned on an unknown planet, which was on the whole, quite a bit better. The planet was quite hospitable, with water and food aplenty, so at least they would not starve.

Frank had spent the last few days tinkering with the communications array and his F.T.L. drive, connecting cables between the two and mumbling to himself as he worked. Wickede had tried to ask him what he was doing but Frank's response was a long string of calculations, so he now left him to get on with whatever he was doing, leaving a plate of food and drinks next to him so at least he didn't starve. From what Snoodgrass had said, when Frank was working on an idea he would often reply to questions with calculations or even in a string of binary numbers, and it wasn't until he finished that he became intelligible again and talked as normally as he ever was going to. Finally Frank looked up from the F.T.L. drive where he had just connected a keyboard and grinned at Wickede.

"I've done it. You need to send a short message, no more than twenty characters."

"Done what?" asked a confused Wickede, not having a clue what Frank was going on about.

"Sorry, didn't I tell you what I was trying to do? Of course I didn't in case it didn't work and I looked stupid. I've connected the communicator to the F.T.L. drive which will work just enough to act as a signal booster. The signal should follow the path we took to get here but I've had to use the final residual Alienbutt essence so we can only send a short message or it won't reach our dimension."

"So we have moved dimension then. I had hoped we had just travelled a really long way," answered Wickede with resignation.

"Don't worry, any rescue mission should be funnelled to where we are and not end up in another dimension entirely. Our transit will have left a tunnel in the fabric of reality and drag a second ship to us like a lodestone. As long as Snoodgrass can follow my designs for the F.T.L. drive we just have to wait here, as long as they get the message. When I realised that the drive may jump dimension I placed a homing beacon on this drive and a locator onto the plans I left with Snoodgrass just in case anything went wrong. I just forgot to tell him about it in the excitement to try the drive out, just an extra bit of insurance in case my lodestone theory doesn't work." Frank smiled apologetically at his slight oversight.

"You're making this up as you go along, aren't you Frank?"

Frank looked sheepish. "Well it is a totally new field of science."

"Do you know for certain we're in another dimension?" asked Wickede.

"Yes," replied Frank. "Almost certainly. Well, quite likely."

Wickede stood up shaking his head. "Let's send a message

and trust that Snoodgrass can follow what the hell you're on about, or I'm going to spend the rest of my life not understanding half of what you say to me. The Omniverse will see us right or leave us for dead, but I'm packing my bags and looking out for an Alienbutt."

A buzzer sounded from the control panel. Wickede walked over to check it out.

"Let's send the message quick. We've got company heading towards the planet. The sensors are picking up three ships, unknown origin."

CHAPTER 17

A Strange Meeting.

INTERSTELLAR NEWS CHANNEL 9.
NEWS FLASH.

In the wake of the Federal Navy's defeat at the Dagnabbit system, the security council of the Federation today announced the appointment of a new Grand Admiral to take over what is being referred to as the Coffee Bean war. Grand Admiral Bush Jr. has promised a swift resolution to the conflict and ordered the conscription of all independent Federation member navies to bolster his forces. General Jee has been placed in charge of all security forces within the Inner Systems by the Federation Security Council and given the power to order martial law and use deadly force against any who show support for the Ick traitors.

Alienbutt stood staring at the small robot. It was about two feet tall and roughly human shaped. The smooth oval head was featureless apart from a single robotic eye at the centre in a dull silver colour like the rest of its body. Snoodgrass stood next to him with a grin on his face.

"To help you out we've fitted the robotic spy probe that received Wickede's message into a robot body and updated its programming. It will be able to interact with the ship's computer and take you to the exact spot where it received the message for you to set course. This robot is state of the art but has a level of conscious thought that is unique, and we still don't understand how it came by this."

Alienbutt didn't look convinced about his new shipmate, having a natural dislike of robots of any kind.

"I thought Admiral Frederick said the thing was stir-crazy, Snoodgrass?"

"Not at all Piestoff, it's just a bit odd because of its ability to think for itself. It will be a big help as we've fitted it with loads of little tricks for all eventualities and it has a high artificial intelligence too."

Alienbutt turned to look at the ship he was to fly. Here he was happy; a small forty foot Interstellar Raider. The ship was sleek, fast and manoeuvrable with enough fire power to offer good defence against all but the largest ships. The ground crew had just finished loading the hold with equipment that they hoped would cover any problems that might arise. For the last two hours the head of the development team had run through the workings of the F.T.L. drive with Alienbutt, and after hearing all about its believed workings and how they thought it should react, Alienbutt had finally asked where the start and stop button was and then walked off to ensure that the whiskey had been safely secured.

As he stood inspecting the last of the cargo to be loaded

with Snoodgrass he watched the robot spy probe walking up the ramp onto the ship, It walked with the uncomfortable gait of a toddler who had just found its feet, always looking like it was about to fall over.

"Does that robot thing have an identity number, Snoodgrass?"

Snoodgrass looked over to where it was just disappearing into the ship. "It's taken to wanting to be called Kirk, by all accounts." Snoodgrass shrugged. "Are you certain that you don't want a co-pilot, Piestoff? There are plenty of pilots who would jump at the chance."

Piestoff shook his head and then grinned. "I'm looking forward to being able to fly without the butt plugs in and if I have anyone along they would only complain."

The last of the supplies was loaded and the hold doors shut. Piestoff turned to his friend and put his hand on his shoulder.

"I've told Grommit and Killashandra to keep an eye on you and make sure that you're looking after yourself, Snoodgrass, I know how you forget to sleep and eat when you get to planning. Now bugger off and let me get going as I'm crap at goodbyes."

Snoodgrass grinned and watched as Piestoff wandered over to the ship and up the ramp. He just prayed that when he saw him next Wickede would be stood next to him.

Alienbutt climbed into the pilot's chair and fired up the engines. Looking over his shoulder and down at the floor, he sighed at the space where Poodles should have been.

"Ya daft dog," he said to himself, smiling sadly.

Lifting off he headed away from the station towards the Ashia Minor sector, the only relatively safe route out of Ick space. The robot Kirk wandered up into the cockpit and stood silent for a moment.

"Are we approaching our destination yet, Sir?" he asked in an electronic voice that Alienbutt knew he would find very annoying as their journey continued.

"We've only been in the air for five minutes, robot," he answered.

"Could you call me by the name Kirk, please, Sir?" he responded, Alienbutt looked around and down at him. He supposed that the Ick made him so small so they wouldn't have to look up at him.

"OK Kirk, but you call me Alienbutt and not Sir, and is there any way to make your voice less robotic?"

Kirk cocked his head to one side as if considering the request.

"I am afraid not, Alienbutt. Could I ask you a question?" Alienbutt nodded as he began to program the flight controls. "Do you like to watch films? I have an extensive range on my hard drive. There's nothing like a film to help pass the time."

Alienbutt looked back at the robot; he instinctively knew that this conversation was going to set the whole tone of their relationship. Kirk pressed on, taking Alienbutt's silence as approval. "I have got all the Star Trek films; we could watch them in order." The robotic voice almost sounded pleading.

Alienbutt looked back at the computer screen and finished setting the auto pilot; he just knew that this would be a long voyage.

"I'll think about it." He had never really watched films. They were mainly a human pastime and only available on pay per view out in the Sloppystool system. Growing up they couldn't afford the holo-screen to watch them on and later he had either been working or drinking so he didn't have the time.

"You will not regret your decision Alienbutt," put in Kirk, almost sounding excited, in a robotic monotone sort of voice.

Over the last five days Alienbutt had watched two of the films a day and realised two things. Firstly he should have asked Snoodgrass how to turn off the robot Kirk, as the bloody thing never stopped talking, especially about Star Trek. Secondly, the films were quite entertaining but the best thing about them was they stopped the robot talking; giving Alienbutt some much needed quiet time. He had plotted a course to avoid any Ick fleets and especially those of the Federation so when his sensors picked up ships entering the system they were in, he quickly began to program the ship's computer for a jump to light speed. Half way through setting the coordinates his ship was hailed. Pausing, he opened communication.

"Commander Alienbutt, if you continue to program your computer to jump to light speed then I will be forced to destroy your ship." Alienbutt finished putting in the co-ordinates.

"I will give you no more warnings Commander. I just want to deliver a message and then you can go about your business."

Alienbutt paused in the act of pressing the button, then moved his finger away. "You had better be quick, I've an appointment with my tailor and he hates it when I'm late."

Alienbutt watched as one of the three ships continued towards him, the others coming to a stop, apparently happy to wait. The ships were about the same size as an Ick dreadnought but more sleek and looking like they were built for speed, but Alienbutt had no doubt that they would also pack a punch. He didn't recognise the ships and they carried no markings. Kirk came and stood next to the pilot's chair cocking his head to one side in the gesture he always made when he was considering something.

"It's almost time for Star Trek. Do you think they would like to watch it with us?"

Alienbutt had already learnt that the robot didn't understand sarcasm so he just ignored him as the robot continued to speak.

The radio came back to life, the voice was female but far from being soft and warm managed to convey that a world of pain would be delivered to anyone who didn't do exactly what she said.

"Commander Alienbutt, if you drop your shields and prepare to be beamed aboard our vessel, we can deliver our message to you face to face."

Alienbutt grabbed a bottle of whiskey and dropped the shields. After a few moments he felt the strange sensation that heralded the start of the teleport and then he was in a strange room. He quickly took a drink of the whiskey. It served to settle his stomach and also gave out a "I don't give a damn how big your ship is," message. The room was quite dark with most detail lost in the shadows but he knew at least two other people were in there with him.

"You know, this place could look nice, but you need a few more lights to create a friendlier mood, I know a really good interior designer," he said finally, as the silence dragged on.

"We were told you like to make infantile remarks, Commander Alienbutt," said the female voice from the radio. The voice was even more menacing in the flesh.

"It's just Alienbutt, I don't go into all that formal how big is your title. Now I'm sure you didn't plan all this just to tell me I'm childish." Alienbutt didn't like the sound of her voice. For some reason he felt the malice in her voice was reserved just for him; he took another longer drink from his whiskey bottle.

"You search for the dead Ick leader. We have a message you need to give him," said a second female voice, this one was more friendly sounding. Alienbutt tried to make out details from the shadows but could only just make out two darkened forms.

"How do I give a message to a dead man? I'm afraid I'm

no psychic," asked Alienbutt, unnerved by how much these people seemed to know about what he was doing.

"How about I just shoot you and we not bother with this silliness?" said the first voice, and he could tell she really did want to do that.

"Be nice to our guest," admonished the second person, but still in that friendly voice. "Tell Wickede that the cure lies in what was removed. He has to put it back."

"Well, that's cryptic. Did you write the Book of Ick by any chance, as that's full of that sort of nonsense too?" Alienbutt hated puzzles and word play. Why couldn't people just say what they meant?

"I'm glad we never took a contract on you, Alienbutt," said the second person, chuckling. "Also tell him that the death mark has been removed from his head. Our previous employer has broken the contract and seeks to discover things that are none of his business."

"So you're the Galactica then. Why don't you do the universe a favour and kill your former employer?" asked Alienbutt, becoming even more uncomfortable at being in the same room as the legendary assassins. Alienbutt started to feel the disorientation of the teleport working and then was back aboard his own ship.

"Did you invite them to watch a film with us?" asked Kirk as Alienbutt sat back down in his pilot's chair.

"They don't like Star Trek I'm afraid, it's too scary for them. Look, even the thought of watching it has made them run off." The ships had already sped off and disappeared as they jumped to light speed. Alienbutt gave a huge sigh of relief as the flash that heralded their departure faded away. Again Kirk missed the sarcasm completely and wandered off to the back of the ship muttering about stupid people.

Alienbutt arrived at the co-ordinates set by Snoodgrass and the Ick scientists two days after his meeting with the Galactica ships. Taking up position beside the communication satellite, he began going over his check list and ensuring that everything was ready. Poking his head into the drive room he saw that the F.T.L. drive was still in the same position as when he had been shown it. With a nod to Kirk, who was following him with the check list of tasks they had to do, he moved onto the next item on the list. He wouldn't have bothered with the list but Kirk had been insistent that it be done, and while he followed Alienbutt around with the clipboard, he had shut up about the history of the Klingon Empire and their great operas. The final item on the list was to switch on the computer that would control the drive and set in the co-ordinates that Wickede's message had been sent from. Finally ready, Alienbutt buckled himself into the pilot's chair and opened a bottle of whiskey. Then he sat taking sips, while staring at the large red button now flashing on his flight control panel. He was aware of Kirk talking to him but he had developed the equivalent of a white noise filter, listening on a subconscious level, so able to answer questions if needed while thinking of other things. He would have been surprised to realise that this was an ability used by married men the universe over for thousands of years, an intergalactic survival trait that held true to every species. Finally he reached a decision and pressed the button. For a moment nothing happened, then he was pushed back in his chair as the ship shot forward and disappeared.

General Jee sat reading the report put before him; it was above top secret and had come from an organisation that didn't exist. He knew this for definite, as he was a leading member of the organisation that didn't exist. The spy in the Ick High Command had managed to send information about a mission to rescue Wickede, who wasn't as dead as the organisation hoped. Attached was the information on how to build the engine that was being used, but the spy couldn't help with the fuel additive, although he did state what it was. Jee turned on his computer and typed in the password needed to review all prisoners held within the Federation prison service. Entering a second password, he came to a much shorter list that numbered prisoners on no other list that were held by the Federation. One name stood out. He was in suspended animation and had been held for over six hundred years on a motoring offence. Smiling, he began to write the release forms so the prisoner could be released into the custody of the cybernetics department of the organisation that didn't exist. The organisation would also start building the ship and engine needed so the released prisoner could hunt down and kill Wickede and Alienbutt. By the time the ship was ready the prisoner would be upgraded and reprogrammed into an unstoppable killing machine. General Jee sat back and smiled. Everything was going to plan again, and very soon he would be in a position to act. He would be the first Emperor of the universe and his control would be total. First he would destroy the Ick and then remove the head of his own organisation and any other of the council that could be a threat, and he would rule the universe unchallenged.

CHAPTER 18

Hope and Dream.

INTERSTELLAR NEWS CHANNEL 9.
NEWS FLASH.

As the war against the Ick rebels drags into its tenth month, unrest continues to build as more anti-war protests have been broken up by security forces. With no sign of any gains in the war and static fronts being set up around Ick space and large areas of the Outer Systems, calls for a peace deal are growing. On a number of worlds security forces have been deployed to stem rebel insurgents from seizing control. Now a total of thirty planets have been brought under direct control of the Federal Security Council. This does not include those already controlled by the Coffee Houses.

In the months that Nifty had been in hiding, Mr. Fluffy had been busy. His first job had been to reprogram the ship's medical computer to implant an altered human interface chip into the back of his skull. With that done, he could link in straight to the ship's computer and had quickly altered all security controls to himself, while sending false information to Nifty so as not to alert her of his plans. Reprogramming the sleeping crew to obey him had proved more difficult and for some reason Blackarachnia was immune to his efforts to brainwash him. In need of certain supplies not available on the ship, he had sent a message to the leaders of the Coffee Houses offering a trade. He had revived two of the senior ship's technicians and set them to work building a body suit for him. In a storage hold he had found damaged robotic infantry and battle armour collected over Blackarachnia's career. When finished, within a week or so he would be ready to make his move. Nifty he would hunt down himself but he would allow the Coffee House human to deal with Blackarachnia in return for the materials to build a suit worthy of him, and not the cobbled together one he would have to use to hunt Nifty. Very soon he would be ready to reveal his brilliance to the universe as he claimed it for himself.

Hydroponic sat on the river bank in the shade of a cherry blossom tree that kept shedding pink petals over him as the gentle breeze moved the branches. It was a warm spring morning, just perfect for fishing. He knew that he should be doing something important, but the fish were biting and his keep-net was filling up. Suddenly a large trout poked its head above the water and seemed to look directly at him. This struck him as strange, but when the fish spoke he found it even more so.

"Listen up, my sister Hope is coming to visit you. Listen to what she says."

"I'm going to meet two speaking fish? Wow! You spend your life never meeting one, then two show up in the same day."

"Don't be a lump! I'm not a fish. I just needed an easy way to get into your dream so I could get my sister in here too, so I chose this form to appear and deliver my message. Fish seem to be something that catches your attention."

With that the fish dropped beneath the water's surface and swam off. Hydroponic shrugged his shoulders. The fact he had just seen a talking fish didn't seem odd, and he returned his attention back to watching the float that bobbed around near a clump of reeds by the far bank.

After a few minutes he became aware of a young woman sat beside him. He couldn't seem to focus on what she looked like, or if he could, he instantly forgot when he looked away.

"Hi, I'm Hope," she said in a pleasant tone.

"You don't look like your brother," replied Hydroponic, returning his attention to his float. He was having a great time fishing and was not happy at all the interruptions.

"Dream doesn't usually look like that, but I needed a quiet word with you without the rest of the family finding out, so I needed to get inside your head." Hydroponic considered this a moment and then shrugged. It was strange how in dreams such things didn't freak you out.

"Look, Fate and Destiny really buggered things up so now we are all running around trying to sort things as they happen. Alienbutt shouldn't be here in your reality, but he is and I like him so I'm going to help you all out. Here's what you've got to do when you wake up."

Sitting up in his bunk Hydroponic felt a moment of total disorientation. The dream had been so real, and as he stood up he realised just how real it had been. The floor of his sleeping quarters was covered in pink blossom petals and a large wet keep-net revealed two large rainbow trout. With a grin Hydroponic grabbed the fish and set off to prepare breakfast, then he would change course and head for the new destination given to him in his dream.

Killashandra slumped into the chair and took the drink offered to her by an equally exhausted Captain Noble. A week ago the Federation had sent an invasion force to try and take control of the giant mining operation in the Dulbarn Quadrant of Ashia Minor. Fierce fighting on a dozen worlds and constant space battles had claimed thousands of lives, but the invasion fleet had been destroyed and the stranded Federation armies had surrendered. The majority of the armies were troops conscripted to the war by the Security Council from worlds within the Inner System.

"Well General, you've got a second victory under your belt, and the Federation are still struggling to get their metal supplies to rebuild their robot army," said Captain Noble, taking a seat next to her.

"I wish they would find another leader for out here. This responsibility is killing me. How about I resign and name you the boss? You're way more experienced anyway and this was mainly your battle plan."

"If you even think about doing that to me I'm gonna claim that kill on sight bounty that the Federation placed on you last month," Captain Noble said, grinning at Killashandra. "Anyway my battle plan went butts up after the second day. You made it all up as you went along after that and snatched victory back for us. You're a natural at this, girl, so accept it."

"It was that suicidal charge by Ponnfarr that turned the tide for us. God knows how he came out of that unscathed."

The odd Fo'c'sle pilot had gathered up half a dozen ships and raced to smash a squadron of Federation battle cruisers that were threatening to destroy the shield generators around the main mining complex. His was the only ship to survive, but the destruction of the Federation squadron by them turned the battle. Killashandra scowled as she took another drink.

"When I catch up with that Alienbutt I'm gonna rip him a fifth hole; this is all his fault. He should be commanding us here, not me."

Captain Noble looked at Killashandra and could see her concern for the strange, oddly dressed Alienbutt who had been sent on some top secret mission months ago, and there had been no word of him since.

CHAPTER 19

Cat Suit.

INTERSTELLAR NEWS CHANNEL 9.
NEWS FLASH.

As the first anniversary of the start of the war of the coffee bean passed, rationing of fuel for space travel was increased to include all non-security or essential ships. The latest drive for recycling all non-essential robots and ships reached its monthly target level with a week to spare. The Federation Security Council would like to thank all citizens for their support in the war effort. In an official statement, the Security Council also announced that planets giving support to the rebels will have their supply of coffee beans reassigned to planets loyal to the Federation. Also extra quotas will be given to those planets donating the most to the war effort.

Mr. Fluffy looked at the battle suit. It stood over ten feet in height, and concealed within the metal casing was a large array of weapons. The robotic control unit, when connected to his brain, would be more advanced than anything ever seen before. The only down side to his creation was the lack of equipment that would allow him to relieve himself when he hooked himself up to it, so a more primitive means was needed. Mr. Fluffy would have to wear a nappy. The Federation ship would be with him within twelve hours, so he only had a few hours to wait until he made his move against Nifty. She had been a good pet but he no longer needed her. He was still upset with her anyway for the way she had taken up with the one called Blackarachnia, and so she would pay for her disloyalty.

Nifty walked onto the bridge of the ship and again checked the sensors. For the last few days a feeling of foreboding had been growing, but the sensors showed that everything was normal. The ship was showing the same readings for all systems as it always did, and that, she realised, was what had been bothering her. The ship's systems were showing the exact same base readings that they had each time she checked, always the optimum perfect results. She checked the readouts for the stasis booths from the console and swore. Running back into Blackarachnia's office where she had been sleeping, she grabbed her vid-screen and began to read her message from the Book of Ick. The message had changed; there was another line at the end of it. Cursing, she ran for the door that led to the corridor, she needed to get to Blackarachnia. Racing through the doorway she sensed movement and instinctively dived and rolled as a large robotic arm crashed through the air where her head had been moments before.

"Hello my Nifty, I've come to play, prrrrrr."

Nifty got back to her feet staring in horror at the large

robot with a moulded cat face. Lightning fast, it struck again. Nifty again jumped out of the way, but a glancing blow caught her on her ribs, slamming her into the wall. Pain wracked her side and she now had four gashes from large razor claws on the robotic arm of the cat robot that began to seep blood. The cuts were not deep but they added to the rising panic she felt. Turning in fear, she began to run.

Blackarachnia had known from the moment he had first seen Nifty that she was the one. True, the age gap was large but she still looked real good for being several hundred years old. When they had been introduced and they shook hands he had felt like he had been electrocuted, and knew he must have seemed a total fool, but in the moment of contact a bond had been formed. Now no matter what, he could tell what she was feeling. Even in the stasis booth he could feel it and suddenly he knew she was afraid. He came awake in an instant and began to smash at the lid of the booth. On the second blow the glass shattered and Blackarachnia reached out to open the door. Falling to the floor, he cursed. Hibernation sickness. It would take hours before he even had the energy to walk. Looking around he saw a medical kit and began to crawl towards it. He didn't have hours; he needed to get his body working quickly.

Nifty managed to get half way down the corridor before a blow to her back sent her sprawling again. She came up slower, knowing that at least a couple of ribs were broken and her arm dislocated. The robotic Mr. Fluffy was a few feet away and making a loud purring noise. Putting her hand in the pocket of the combat trousers, she hoped to find something to use as a weapon, anything to help. Instead she pulled out a half used ball of wool that she had been using to knit a scarf. Mr. Fluffy stopped and stood staring at what was in her hand. Being a super-villain in a battle suit was great, but being that super-villain with cat instincts that couldn't be fully suppressed was a problem. He was super intelligent but still deep down inside he was Mrs. Tiddles the cat's little kitten. Without thinking Nifty threw the ball high and to his left and waited for those cat instincts to take over. Both arms came up to catch it as he jumped, spun and twisted. Unable to prevent his reaction he overbalanced and fell backwards with a giant crash. Nifty was off and running again before he even hit the floor.

Geurick Tackful stood on the bridge of his ship. His excitement at the job he was about to start was now approaching fever pitch. The dreadnought was well hidden within an asteroid and would have been missed if they hadn't been given the exact co-ordinates. He had just transported the equipment promised for the trade into the cargo hold of the ship and was awaiting permission to come aboard to get Blackarachnia. The unknown Mr. Fluffy had told him that he was free to hunt down the legendary bounty hunter, but to leave the Nifty Niffler for him to deliver up. He didn't mind this as from the research he had done, Nifty was just some Earth celebrity and not really a challenging hunt for his skills. Picking up the last of his four custom pistols out of the silver case before him, he placed it into a holster across his chest and turned to head for the transporter room. He suppressed the excitement he felt, as he would need total concentration to face the deadly Blackarachnia.

Nifty entered the main cargo hold of the ship. She was feeling light headed but had managed to lose Mr. Fluffy using the trick with the ball of wool. This had given her time to sort out running repairs to her battered body. Popping her arm back had almost caused her to pass out, but at least now she could use both arms again and so had managed to bandage up her ribs. She had first headed for the stasis booths but found Blackarachnia's empty, smashed open from the inside. Her husband was nowhere to be seen. On the floor by the smashed booth were discarded insulin shots and other stimulants. Knowing that her husband was awake and aware that there was trouble made her feel better, as he would be more able to fend for himself than just about anyone, even after just coming out of a stasis booth.

In the centre of the cargo bay was a number of large crates that hadn't been there before, but she didn't have time to ponder this as she heard the clonking of the Fluffy robot heading down the corridor outside. He had caught her by surprise last time, now it was time to repay the favour and show that jumped up little cat who the boss was. Grabbing a tool box from the wall, she ran to find a place to hide while she chose usable weapons.

Blackarachnia walked down the darkened corridor. He had just visited his quarters to gather up his weapons, sunglasses and other tools of his trade. He had shot himself up with as many stimulants as possible and carried a small oxygen tank, yet still felt weak. He knew something had gone seriously wrong and that was confirmed when a figure stepped out of the shadows further down the corridor.

"Blackarachnia, I've so looked forward to meeting you." The man stepped forward into a pool of light from the emergency lighting that was operating while the ship had been sitting hidden. Blackarachnia recognised the young Federation assassin Geurick Tackful.

"Look, boy, I'm not in the mood for signing autographs so run along and play somewhere else." He had always suspected that one day he would have to face the assassin, but knew at the moment he wasn't in any condition to face him in a fair fight.

Geurick smiled at the insult. "I'm not going to just kill you, old man, I'm going to batter you all over the ship first and make you beg for your life. The whole thing will be recorded and the universe will witness your death at my hand. I challenge you to hand to hand combat."

When bounty hunters had disagreements that couldn't be settled any other way, they would issue challenges and the code of honour of the hunters would mean neither would break the code, even if it meant death.

Blackarachnia put his hands into his coat pocket, his fingers slipping into the knuckle dusters that he always kept in there.

"Well, boy, you talk a good fight, throwing down the hunter challenge like that, but you're not nearly ready to face me and live, last chance to move."

A drawn out fight would only end one way, he knew that, so Blackarachnia would have to play it sly. Pulling his hands out of his pocket he placed the oxygen mask over his face and took a deep breath, while with his other hand he unclipped a small vial from his belt. As Geurick moved forward he threw it on the ground between them, releasing a greenish gas. Geurick stopped in his tracks, choking, while Blackarachnia, holding his breath, ran forward to smash him in the face. Geurick dropped as if poleaxed. Blackarachnia took another breath of the oxygen and looked down at the unconscious assassin.

"Alienbutt essence, boy, works every time, and you're no hunter to be able to issue that challenge." He considered killing the assassin where he lay, but decided against it. There was a time he would have slit his throat without a thought, but he must be getting old and soft. Walking on, he continued to search for Nifty and answers to what was happening.

185

Mr. Fluffy strode into the cargo bay. He knew Nifty was hiding in here; he could smell her, but with the arrival of the Federation ship and their assassin he would have to cut short his play time and kill Nifty quickly. Walking down the steps to the floor of the bay he scanned the room looking for his prey. Three steps from the bottom, the step gave way and he fell forward. Instantly his arm shot out and he grabbed a metal pipe to steady himself. Looking down he saw the step had been cut through with a laser torch. Gripping the pipe work with enough force to crush it, he began to pull himself up, and then he heard a whistle from above. Looking up he saw Nifty thirty feet above him on a gantry and before he realised what was happening she placed a live electric cable to the pipe he gripped. Thousands of volts of electricity shot down the pipe and Mr. Fluffy found himself blown across the bay to crash into the far wall, his metallic hand and lower arm melted in seconds. Nifty nimbly jumped down and advanced towards the battered and smoking robotic Fluffy.

"Here kitty kitty, I've not finished yet," she said sweetly. The robotic suit started to move and Nifty stopped, then watched as Fluffy sprang nimbly back to his feet.

"You are finished my Nifty, but will suffer for that, ppprrrrr." Fluffy looked down at the melted stump of his robotic arm. It was a prototype. The next one would be insulated against electricity. Cat quick he raised his other arm and bullets flew from a small rail gun mounted to the lower arm, but Nifty was faster, diving to the side and taking cover behind the newly delivered crates. Mr. Fluffy screamed in rage as his gunfire accidentally ripped apart his precious cargo. He was angry and too eager to make the kill; he was making mistakes. He strode around the crates intent on stamping Nifty into the floor. Instead he came face to face with a crouching Nifty armed with a laser cannon that she had unpacked from one of the crates. He had a second to register this before she fired, blowing the head off his robotic suit. Again he was thrown back and the ruined suit hit the floor to slide until it hit a pile of engine spare parts. Nifty stood and hefted the cannon. The weapon was large and she struggled to hold it, but she advanced on the ruined robotic suit of Mr. Fluffy.

Then the doors to the cargo bay opened. Nifty swung the gun ready to fire but saw Blackarachnia leaning against the door.

"Next time you gas me and chuck me in stasis, could you give me a day to recover before I have to go running around the ship? I'm not as young as I used to be."

He staggered forward and started down the steps. Nifty dropped the gun and ran over to him. She ran into his arms at the bottom of the stairs and stood, enjoying just being back with him for a moment. Then she saw movement at the doorway from the corner of her eye. Instinctively she spun Blackarachnia around and pushed him back just before something hit her in the chest, lifting her off her feet.

Blackarachnia landed on the floor and looked up to see Nifty lifted off her feet, blood spraying from her chest. Without thought he had his pistol out of its holster and pointed at the doorway, so when Geurick came into sight he took two shots in the upper chest and fell back through the doorway. Blackarachnia scrambled over to where Nifty lay, blood flowing freely from the wound in her chest. He had only minutes to save her. Scooping her up, he headed for the ship's runabout that was stored in the cargo bay so there was more room in the hanger for extra fighter ships. Opening the doors to the small ship he carried the already unconscious Nifty inside. His only chance to save her was to get her into the mobile stasis booth aboard the runabout until he could get her to proper medical help. Once there, they could use a medical stasis field over the injuries and nano probes to heal the injuries.

Geurick felt pain like never before. He had been hit in the upper chest and shoulder, smashing his collar bone. Taking a small pot of powder from a pouch on his belt, he sprinkled it on the wounds, gritting his teeth as the powder burnt the wounds closed and stopped the blood flow. Almost passing out, he was brought back to the here and now by large explosions that rocked the ship, then his communicator came to life.

"Commander Tackful, a small runabout has just taken off from the enemy dreadnought. Do you want us to destroy it?"

Geurick got to his knees. He had underestimated the bounty hunter. He had believed the stories of the gentleman hunter who always fought fair, but the truth was Blackarachnia was a pub scrapper who would use any trick going to give him the edge.

"Beam me aboard now, I will destroy the ship myself," he ordered. Blackarachnia had been much more devious than he thought he would be. The gas attack had been unexpected, but now he would shoot him out of space and it would be done.

Blackarachnia jumped into the pilot's seat and fired up the engines on the runabout. Manoeuvring the ship into the centre of the cargo bay, he charged up the forward cannons and fired at the outer doors, blowing them out in an explosion that rocked the entire ship. Looking out to open space through the ruined doors, he retracted the ship's landing gear and set off. As soon as he was airborne he saw the Federation frigate begin to move to intercept him. He knew he would have to be at his best to outrun this ship, and he was far from that, and he didn't stand a chance in a stand up fight. Angling away from the enemy ship he hoped the pilot wasn't very good at steering in such a close chase. Then there came a flash from ahead of him as a second ship jumped out of light speed. Blackarachnia began to turn the ship from the new arrival, cursing the universe in general.

Hydroponic jumped out of light speed and took in the scene before him in an instant. Ignoring the runabout, he sped for the Federation ship, opening fire. As explosions battered the ship it swerved away from its intended prey and quickly jumped to light speed, not wanting to face this new arrival that obviously had it outgunned. Hydroponic watched the Federation ship leave and opened up communications as he swung his ship back around.

"Blackarachnia, let's get you out of the wee daft ship and out of here before that Federation ship comes back with some friends."

"Hydroponic?" asked Blackarachnia, amazed at his old partner's arrival. "Help me, Nifty's hurt, I think she's dying."

CHAPTER 20

An Unexpected Visitor.

INTERSTELLAR NEWS CHANNEL 9.
NEWS FLASH.

As the war drags on and sanctions on travel continue to affect the trade within the Federation, shortages of non-essential items are becoming critical. Professor Squegal Quinch, head of economics at the Rorcthope planet university has warned that the entire infrastructure of the Federation could collapse within months unless normal trading was resumed. In response, General Jee ordered his execution for high treason. Riots that ensued at the university were put down with a targeted nuclear strike.

General Jee has now ordered a rounding up of all academics and students to weed out dissident elements.

Wickede sat staring at the sky, waiting. Every evening at this time, a huge flock of large orange birds would fly over, heading for the great lake in the valley below. In the six months since Alienbutt had arrived, the two had sat every evening and watched the spectacle. Finally Alienbutt trudged up the hill to sit next to his friend.

"You're late, Piestoff, almost missed them."

"I'm sure they wouldn't care, as I've sat and watched them every evening for months."

"You have no appreciation of natural beauty, Piestoff. Look around you it's a stunning planet we're on."

Alienbutt looked around at the hills and rolling grasslands that surrounded them, with thick forests covering the valley floors down to the great lakes that seemed to be all around.

"Too many hills to walk up and the trees get in the way," said Alienbutt dismissing the subject.

"Well, you could have stayed in camp each evening and watched Kirk's film show."

"Frank says we're ready to go first thing in the morning as long as her Majesty doesn't change her mind again," continued Alienbutt, ignoring Wickede's last comment. They would have been back home weeks ago, but their host, who had helped Wickede out before Alienbutt's arrival, had kept postponing their departure date with one excuse after another and Wickede insisted it would be rude to depart without her leave.

They had ended up in a different dimension Alienbutt had been informed on his arrival. Here, a giant frog type species lived in this part of space. They were a peaceful species and couldn't understand this concept of war, but one of the Queen's daughters was fascinated by the lives of Wickede and his companions. She had already convinced her mother to delay them, postponing their departure to hear more stories of their strange lives.

191

The flock of birds flew over, thousands of the giant creatures all heading to the lakes for the evening. Despite what Alienbutt said to Wickede, he loved to watch this daily flight, fascinated by the fact that they never flew into each other, but always hoping that if he watched often enough he would see that collision. As the last of the birds finished flying over, Wickede stood up and took a final look around as the shadows began to lengthen.

"Frank is sure he has a way to sort out the coffee addiction problem when we get back. I didn't understand a word of what he said though," said Alienbutt as he too stood up.

"I never know what he's on about, Piestoff, but I trust that he's right in what he says."

The cure for coffee was so simple. It wasn't a matter of finding some agent to remove the addictive quality of the bean but just a matter of putting back something the Coffee Houses had removed through genetic manipulation. Caffeine was that magic element that occurred naturally in the plant, a natural stimulant, but somehow the producers had discovered if they decaffeinated the plant and bean then you had the most addictive drug ever seen in space. Frank had a theory that the reason that production had dropped was the plant trying to repair itself. The genetically modified plant was reverting to its natural state and producing the caffeine again, so the Coffee Houses were destroying all caffeine infected crops.

The two walked down the hill back to the compound which had been their base. Alienbutt's repaired ship sat on the launch pad. It had suffered extensive electrical damage in the F.T.L. jump, and Frank had spent over two months rebuilding the flight computer, and then to Alienbutt's disgust he then repaired the robot Kirk. Off to one side stood three strange-looking sphere-like ships of the frog people, floating just above the ground. Frank was fascinated by the organic quality and technology that the frogs used and had studied it extensively, with plans to try and duplicate their science when they returned home. As they entered the compound, Frank came running out of the building where they stayed. He saw Wickede and Alienbutt and ran over to them.

"A ship just appeared. All the readings from that sector of space say it's from our dimension." He stopped before them, looking excited, but confused by the ship's appearance.

"It has the F.T.L. Drive? But how did they get the fuel to make the jump?" asked Wickede, confused, walking towards the building to look at the sensor reports. Frank shrugged at Alienbutt and then followed after Wickede.

"It's heading this way so we should know within the hour," he shouted to Wickede as the Ick leader entered the building.

Wickede and Alienbutt stood in the centre of the camp, each holding pulse-rifles. Wickede had sent the frog people to hide in the forests until the occupants of the new ship were known, while Frank sat in the pilot's chair of Alienbutt's ship ready to take off, Kirk standing beside him.

"Hope whoever they are they've got whiskey aboard, Wick."

Wickede shook his head. "After that two day hangover you had the other week you want to start drinking again?"

A flare in the darkening sky heralded the ship entering the atmosphere; both adjusted their stance and hefted their guns.

"Only a small ship then, so won't have much room for storage, Piestoff," Wickede said, matter of factly.

The two watched the ship swing about to erratically head for the camp, which was lit up with flood lights as twilight advanced to full night.

"Well either he's a crap pilot, or he must have lost his computer and controls the same as we did," observed Wickede as the ship got closer.

"Just hope Frank's right about him losing his guns too if he's not friendly, or as cool as this looks, us standing out here is going to be a bloody stupid thing to do," added Alienbutt, rolling his shoulders to relieve the ache there.

"Did you ever watch the old Earth movie called Butch Cassidy and the Sundance Kid? There's a great bit at the end," started Wickede,

"If they died I don't want to know," cut in Alienbutt. Wickede stopped talking and looked guilty as they watched the ship get closer.

"They did die, didn't they? What a great comparison to make," said Alienbutt, looking at Wickede with a silent accusation in his eyes. "You really know how to make me feel better. He's not slowing down. I think standing here is gonna backfire, Wickede," Alienbutt said, starting to sound worried.

"He will, or he's gonna crash the ship big time," Wickede replied, not sounding convinced. "He'll hit the brakes soon."

Both continued to watch for another few seconds as the ship loomed larger, then as one, they turned and ran as the nose of the ship hit the far side of the camp, sending up a shower of earth as the ship started to plough through the ground towards them.

Alienbutt got to his knees coughing. Dust and soil filled the air, but the ground had stopped moving. Picking up his rifle he stood up and peered through the gloom. Half the floodlights that were set up around the camp had stopped working or been smashed. As the dust began to settle, he made out the shape of the half buried ship and over to his right Wickede, who was also getting to his feet.

"She's a Federation scout ship, Wickede. How the hell did they get F.T.L. technology?" Alienbutt shouted over to his friend. The door on the side of the ship began to open but stopped half way. Smoke and fumes billowed out. With two great metallic bangs the occupant knocked open the door the rest of the way and walked out. Through the smoke and dust, Alienbutt struggled to see the figure. He looked about the same size as him, but bulked much larger in the hazy light. Then Alienbutt's wrist communicator burst to life. It was Frank.

"Look out, it's a cyborg! And Alienbutt, you're not going to believe this, but it's half Alienbutt."

"Who put that bloody hill there?" demanded the booming voice of the cyborg. Turning towards Alienbutt, he raised his arm as if to point, and opened fire with a small rail gun attached to the arm.

Wickede was already running. As he saw the cyborg raise his arm to point at Alienbutt, he jumped. Crashing into his friend, they both went flying just as the bullets from the cyborg's arm-mounted gun cut through the space where Alienbutt had been stood. Wickede got to his knees and brought up his rifle.

"Come on Alienbutt, let's shoot this thing and then get the hell out of here." Alienbutt nodded and brought his rifle to bear. As the cyborg came into view again, both fired. The cyborg was lifted off its feet and fell backwards. Wickede stood up and inspected a large rip in his trousers. He was just about to speak when four loud pops came from the direction of the cyborg. Alienbutt jumped up and grabbed his arm, dragging him away from the crashed ship and the cyborg.

"Wickede, it's a fart attack. Run!" screamed Alienbutt in alarm. Both started to run as a green gas cloud began to expand from the area where the cyborg had landed.

CHAPTER 21

The Battle of the Farts.

INTERSTELLAR NEWS CHANNEL 9.
NEWS FLASH.

News is coming in of a large mobilisation of Federation forces for a new offensive against the Ick and Outer System traitors. Unconfirmed reports state that a number of Ick positions have been overrun and at least one of the rebel ringleaders has been killed, but a name has not been released. In fierce fighting all along the Ashia Minor belt, reports state large gains for the Federation forces.

Wickede was half dragged by Alienbutt towards the ship, the dust and smoke from the cyborg's ship's crash gave them cover, and added to this was a rapidly expanding green fog from the cyborg's fart attack, reducing visibility to only a few feet in any direction. Alienbutt had a natural filtration system in his nose that, while leaving him light-headed from the cyborg Alienbutt's fumes, didn't leave him almost unconscious like Wickede. Pressing a button on his wrist communicator he looked down at the Ick leader who was quickly losing all consciousness.

"Frank, send out Kirk to get Wickede off me, then when we're all aboard you take off!"

"He's on his way now to you, Alienbutt. The ship is prepped and ready to go."

Reaching the bottom of the ramp to the ship, Alienbutt put down Wickede and looked back towards where the cyborg was appearing through the haze. Hefting his gun he took aim and fired, spinning the cyborg around, but this time it didn't go down. Kirk toddled down the ramp and grabbed Wickede's wrist and began to drag the now unconscious Ick up into the ship.

"Alienbutt, I'm ready to take off as soon as you give the word," cut in Frank's voice from over the wrist communicator. Alienbutt stood on the bottom of the ramp peering through the mist, trying to spot the cyborg.

"Let's get out of here, Frank," he replied, taking another step up the ramp, still watching the haze for sign of the cyborg. The gloom was lit up; Alienbutt looked to see a large missile heading towards the ship, only to explode as it hit the energy shields about ten feet out from the ship. Frank had been taking no chances of the cyborg damaging the ship, but still the blast knocked Alienbutt over. He fell, rolling from the ramp just as the ship began to take off, and the ramp closed.

Getting to his knees, he saw the cyborg, a missile launcher upon his shoulder, aiming at the ship. Alienbutt grabbed his rifle and fired, again hitting the cyborg so that he fired the missile wide. At such close range the shields couldn't take too many hits before buckling, but more importantly, he didn't want find out how good a pilot Frank was when dealing with the blasts from the explosions that could still make him lose control and crash at such a low altitude. The ship was in the air now and moving off, but Alienbutt knew it wasn't safe from a ground attack, and he didn't know what other weapons the cyborg had.

"Alienbutt, I'll swing around and come back for you," came Frank's voice over the wrist communicator.

"No! Those missiles it's firing could bring down the ship. You need to get Wickede and the cure for coffee back to the Ick. Just work out a way to come back for me once you win."

"But Alienbutt," Frank began.

"That's an order, Frank. I'm pulling the rank that Wickede gave me. Now punch the button and go," shouted Alienbutt. He saw the cyborg again taking aim at the ship and emptied the last of his ammunition at him as the ship shot off into the sky.

Pressing a button on the belt of his codpiece, he released the butt-plugs safety, allowing the free escape of fumes. He had read about his people's culture and in particular the single combat challenge of a fart battle to the death. Pulling out a handful of dried Garogian Chillies from a pouch on his belt, he stuffed them in his mouth. With his mouth burning and eyes watering from the strongest known chillies, he prepared for his challenge.

The cyborg cursed as the ship escaped. Scanning around, it picked up the life-form that had been left behind and smiled. It was crouching down now so the cyborg moved around to begin his approach from behind it. Just as the cyborg reached down to grab Alienbutt he let rip! A gas cloud enveloped the cyborg's outstretched hand, blistering the flesh. Recoiling in pain, he was hit by a second and then a third blast as Alienbutt switched between butt holes for his attack. The flesh of his hand and lower arm began to blacken and blister. Stepping back, the cyborg swung his leg forward and aimed a kick to the ribs that sent the crouching Alienbutt flying through the air. Alienbutt landed heavily, knocking the air from his lungs. Rolling over he saw the cyborg approaching again.

"You took me by surprise there Piestoff, an effective move, but you should have aimed your farts at my face," the cyborg said in his growling metallic voice.

"I'll remember that for my next shot," gasped Alienbutt, getting up onto one knee, still struggling for breath. "You seem to have the advantage on introductions." Alienbutt needed more time to get his breath back and hoped the cyborg would take the bait and stop to answer him. The cyborg obliged, stopping about six feet away and grinning down at Alienbutt.

"Don't you recognise your old man, boy? I know it's been a long time. The body's a bit different, I admit, but they didn't touch the face."

Alienbutt shook his head in horror; he was gazing into a face he remembered from the pictures his mother kept.

"Piestoff, I am your father!" the cyborg said as he moved forward and reached with his metallic arm and picked up Alienbutt, bringing them face to face.

"No!" screamed Alienbutt, and swung his head forward, headbutting the cyborg's face, breaking the nose. With a snarl of rage, Bigrip Alienbutt threw his son to the floor and spun around to let rip with all four butts. Alienbutt felt the flesh on his back and left arm begin to burn as the toxic fumes hit, and screamed at the sudden pain. Being so close to a fart attack by an accomplished Alienbutt put a whole new element to the result. The difference between an ordinary Alienbutt fart and a fart attack was equivalent to a male lion nipping a cub to tell it to bugger off, and that same lion going for a zebra that it's decided would make a great dinner. It wasn't just about the smell; for the first six foot range of the gas spurt it was acidic and able to melt steel plate.

"Alienbutt, we're making the jump now. I promise I'll come back for you." Frank's voice sounded distorted as it came through the half-melted wrist communicator. Bigrip grabbed Alienbutt again with a snarl, lifting him off the floor, and threw him across the camp to slam into the side of the crashed ship. Alienbutt's body worked on instinct. He scrambled under the broken wing of the ship, feeling the heat blast of another round of Bigrip farts hitting the side of the ship where he had landed as Bigrip started to light his farts, creating an instant flame thrower of terrifying proportions. A metallic arm reached under the wing and dragged Alienbutt out, the earth and stone scraping his already injured back. Bigrip stood over his son, grinning down at him as Alienbutt battled to stay conscious. In one last attempt with his failing energy, Alienbutt struggled to free the pistol in his hip holster. As he pulled it clear, Bigrip grabbed a large piece of the ship's wreckage and brought it down, severing the hand at the wrist. Alienbutt gritted his teeth, refusing to allow the scream to come out. He stared up at his father, a look of defiance on his face.

"I still win. Wickede is home free and has the cure for coffee," Growled Alienbutt, battling to remain conscious, but knowing that he was about to die.

"You're game, boy, when I left you were still in your egg and not hatched. I'm proud of you but now it's time to finish this." Bigrip pointed the metallic arm at Alienbutt and a gun came out of the side of the forearm. "I'll finish it quick for you. Just know it's nothing personal against you, I'm just following my programming." He smiled down at his son, then his head disappeared in a spray of blood and gore. After a moment the body collapsed down on itself. Alienbutt blinked trying to clear his vision of blood as he wondered what happened.

He began to lose consciousness, and as he fell into a well of darkness, he saw the face of the frog princess, Isme, loom over him, Wickede's gun in her hands. He heard her voice following after him.

"Your friends have gone Alienbutt, returned to your space, but you're not alone. You won't die on your own, I promise."

Carefully the other frog people advanced and after dressing the worst of his wounds lifted the unconscious Alienbutt and carried him gently away.

Hydroponic sat looking at the sleeping Blackarachnia. He had been forced to sedate his old friend. Always the ice-cold hunter in total control, now Blackarachnia was close to breaking with the thought of losing his wife. Standing up, Hydroponic walked through to his sleeping quarters and lifted the lid on an ancient box sat on a small shelf by his bed. A strange white powder was within; it seemed to almost glow. The Great Ones at the temple called it Mfkzt, a product of some secret rite involving gold. This was the secret of the lost Empire of Sinai and the High Priestess Hethor, Queen of the West. Here was the power to regenerate the body, near immortality if just used on himself, but to heal someone with Nifty's injuries? It could take the entire contents of the box and the contents could not be replaced.

Placing the box back, he walked through to Blackarachnia and the stasis booth where his wife lay frozen in time, just minutes away from death if the lid was opened. It was worth a try to save her and he just hoped there was enough powder that there may be a little left for himself. They were a couple of days from the Hunters Home, the large space station that was the central base of the Outer System bounty hunters. Once there they could begin treatment on Nifty and with luck, save her life. There was, however, one small thing that worried him. Between him and the space station was the small matter of a very large Federation war fleet that would possibly be heading for the station right now.

CHAPTER 22

The Return.

INTERSTELLAR NEWS CHANNEL 9.
NEWS FLASH.

News is still coming in of crushing defeats for the Ick rebels. Grand Admiral Bush Jr. is expected to announce the start of the final push in the next few days. Unconfirmed reports claim that the commander of the Second Fleet of the Ick Navy has been captured and the fleet destroyed during fierce fighting over the last week.

Grommit lay on the hard bunk within the cell. Since being captured she had been treated quite well. Her broken arm had been strapped and the cuts to her face treated. Three guards stood watch over her, showing that they were taking no chances even though the energy shield cell was practically escape-proof.

The doors to the holding area slid open and someone walked in. The guards' stances became even more alert in response to the new arrival. Grommit glanced over and saw a tall muscular figure dressed in the uniform of the E.D.F. officers. Dark green combat trousers with a platinum moulded breastplate and crimson red cloak pinned to the shoulders, the hood of the cloak was pulled up, casting his face in shadow. Grommit, though, didn't need to see the face to know who the newcomer was.

"Why General, so nice of you to visit." The tone of her voice left little doubt that the sight of him was no pleasure.

"Little sister, it appears that you chose the wrong side again. Now you will face trial for treason, but I will ensure that you don't get the death sentence. I think life with hard labour would be more fitting." General Jee stood close to the cell and pulled back the hood of his cloak. "Or maybe selling you into slavery with a behaviour chip implanted would be fun."

Grommit slowly got up off the bunk and walked over until she was inches from her older brother and just the force field of the cell separated them.

"Why don't you get them to drop this barrier and then I'll show you what I think?" she hissed at him.

Jee stared into the eyes of his younger sister and could see the murder in them.

"I take it you're still mad at me for killing our parents and placing the blame on you, then?" He took a couple of steps back as Grommit threw herself at the force field. Electricity shot over her body and threw her back, but again she launched herself forward. Jee was impressed at the pain she was enduring in her rage to get to him. Turning his back to her, he walked past the guards.

"Subdue her," he ordered. Each of the guards pulled clear an electro-batton and advanced. As the force field of the cell was lowered they rushed in to rain blows down on the unarmed Fo'c'sle commander. At first she tried to fight, knocking one guard off his feet and breaking the nose of a second, but it wasn't long before she lay face down on the floor, bleeding and unable to move. Jee then walked forward again. Kneeling next to Grommit, he carefully turned her over and supported her head, cradling her almost gently

"It took me two weeks to break Father and make him beg for his life. I so hope you hold out longer. Don't disappoint me." With that he stood up and turned to one of the guards. "Ensure a video of this is leaked to the Ick Command. Let's see if they try a rescue mission." Then he walked out without a backward glance.

A small Interstellar Raider class ship appeared in a giant flash of rainbow light. This sector of space was empty apart from an old relay satellite, so no one saw the impressive display. The ship sped on for a short time, but then came to a stuttering stop close to the satellite. Inside Professor Frank ran around with a fire extinguisher spraying computer consoles as they sparked and smoked, burnt out by the use of the F.T.L. drive. Finally satisfied that there was no further risk of fire, he checked on the still unconscious Wickede, before walking over to a large lead box. Opening the lid he lifted out the robot Kirk and flipped a switch on the back of his neck. After a brief whirring noise, the robot came to life.

"It appears that your box idea worked, Professor. Should

we watch a film to celebrate?"

"Soon, Kirk. I need you to send a message to the Ick to come pick us up." The robot seemed to consider this for a minute before it again spoke.

"Done, I remote connected to my old relay satellite to boost my signal. There was an Ick dreadnought hiding in the asteroid belt of Big Rock waiting for our return. It will be here in a few minutes."

Frank breathed a sigh of relief. They were back, although leaving Alienbutt didn't feel right. He would work nonstop until he could find a way to get back for him. He looked over to where the leader of the Ick lay. He still looked incredibly green, but the effects of the cyborg Alienbutt gas would soon start to wear off.

The star system was a hive of activity. Giant mobile stardocks had been brought up by the Ick for the repair of the battered fleets that had been battling along the western front of Ashia Minor. Killashandra and her command had been sent back from the front line for repairs and refitting. Her dreadnought command ship limped into one of the giant stardocks. Only two of the five great engines that powered her were operational and a giant tear down the starboard side showed the effects of being rammed by a Federation ship. Under normal conditions the ship would have been scrapped, but they didn't have the ships to spare, so they would patch it up the best they could. As the ship came to a stop and large docking clamps pinned it into position, the surviving crew headed for the hangar bay and transfered to the large space station where they would spend the next week before being reassigned. That was provided the Federation did not launch another offensive.

Killashandra took a final look at the view screen of the ship before leaving the bridge, looking out at the hundred or so ships in the system. Most of them carried damage and she prayed the Federation did not push its advantage, as before her were the entire Ick reserves for the Ashia Minor sector. She turned, expecting to see Captain Noble or Jack Lantern, both constant companions since she had taken over command after the battle at Dagnabbit, but she then remembered that Captain Noble had been evacuated with the seriously injured the day before, while Jack had fallen four days earlier, leading a relief fleet, desperately trying to punch a way through to the Zaldarn System and the besieged second fleet. With the loss of Grommit with that fleet, she now found herself as the Ick Commander for the whole Ashia Minor sector and second only to the giant Duke Ramboe. Not for the last time, she prayed for Alienbutt's return so she could kill him, ever so slowly and painfully for getting her into this predicament.

Snoodgrass sat in his office viewing fresh reports. The latest Federation offensive had finally been stopped, but the losses had been extensive. The whole second fleet under Commander Grommit had been lost; it had taken the entire Ick reserves to prevent a total collapse of the western front. As it was, they had lost eight systems, including two large production centres. It had been thought that Grommit had been killed in the fighting but a video had surfaced showing that she had been captured. Commander Kali had already been to see him about staging a rescue mission, but the truth was that they didn't have the strength and both knew it.

Snoodgrass was brought out of his musings by an incoming message. He was on the verge of ordering the abandoning of a number of systems as they didn't have the fleet left to hold such a large front. If this was news of another Federation offensive, then it could be the beginning of the end for the war. Taking a moment to compose himself, he pressed the button to accept the call.

"Snoodgrass, I'm forwarding you the chemical formula for the cure for coffee addiction. I want it releasing and transmitted immediately on every frequency, and forwarding to all agents in the Federation. Then I want every ship we have mobilisied. I will be with you within three days and then our Empire strikes back!"

Snoodgrass stood up in disbelief. "Wickede?"

"I'm back, my old friend. Your rescue mission worked," answered Wickede grimly. Snoodgrass, though, picked something up in his voice, a pain that he hadn't voiced.

"And Alienbutt?" he asked in dread.

There was a long pause before Wickede replied.

"He didn't make it back. I don't know if he survived, but Frank is already working on a way to get back for him."

Snoodgrass slumped back into his chair, his joy at the return of Wickede evaporated.

AND NOW YOU'RE THINKING: "WHAT SORT OF BLOODY ENDING IS THAT? WHERE IS BOOK TWO!!"

OR

YOU'RE THINKING: "THANK GOD THAT'S OVER."

Whatever, here ends book one of the Alienbutt Saga, The War of the Coffee Bean. In book two (The Rise of Mr. Fluffy) I'm sure things will happen but I don't have a clue what, although Mr. Fluffy has confirmed that he will be back, but demands a bigger part and extra tuna.

Thanks for reading ;)

Special thanks to Hein Goemans (it's his fault), Anna Bouch, Michael Harp, Sandra Morton and Si Barsby and my other friends on FB for all their support.

To my wife (who refuses to read this, as it's silly) and family, thank you for all the support you always give me.